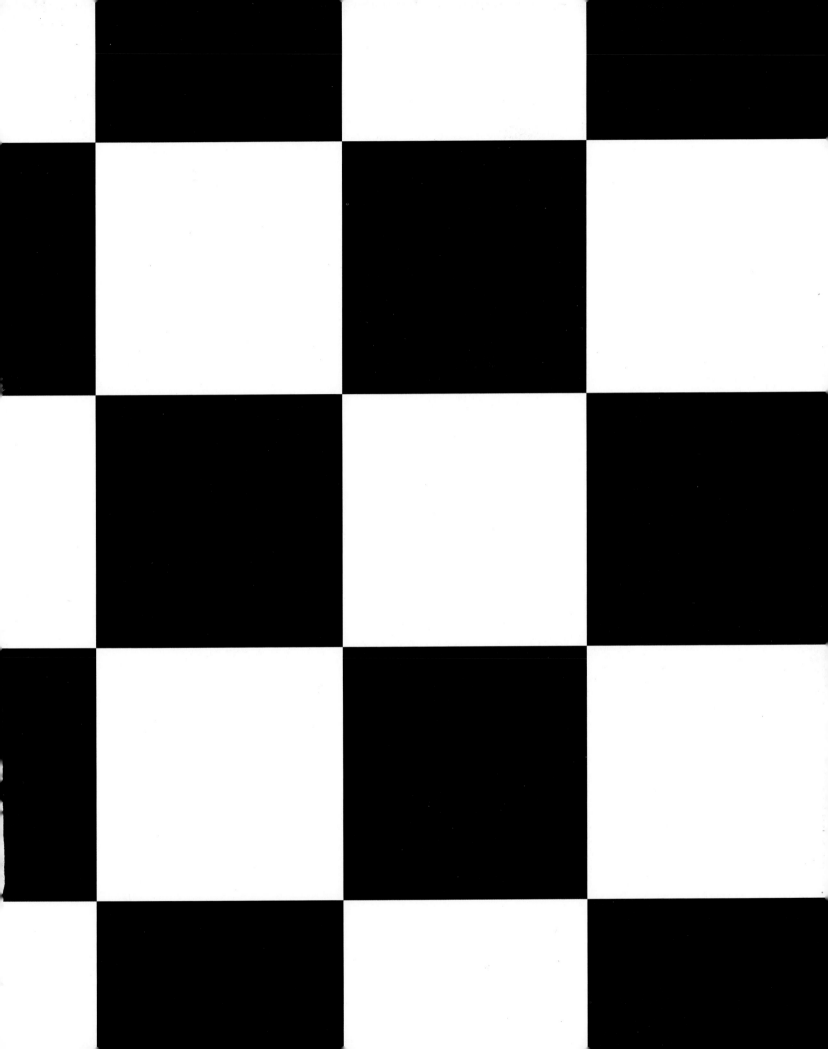

INSIDE
FORMULA ONE 1996:
THE GRAND PRIX
TEAMS

JON NICHOLSON AND
MAURICE HAMILTON

MACMILLAN

First published 1996 by Macmillan

an imprint of Macmillan Publishers Ltd
25 Eccleston Place, London SW1W 9NF
and Basingstoke

Associated companies throughout the world

ISBN 0 333 67851 6

1 3 5 7 9 8 6 4 2

A CIP catalogue record for this book is available from
the British Library.

Photographic reproduction by Aylesbury Studios, Bromley, Kent

Printed and bound in Great Britain by BPC Consumer Books Limited, Bristol,
a member of The British Printing Company Ltd

Note: The statistics given at the start of each chapter

are correct to the start of the 1996 season

CONTENTS

ARROWS

ARROWS

ARROWS

DRIVERS:

JOS VERSTAPPEN (NETHERLANDS)

RICARDO ROSSET (BRAZIL)

TEAM PRINCIPAL • TOM WALKINSHAW

CHIEF DESIGNER • ALAN JENKINS

CAR • ARROWS FA17

ENGINE • HART V10

FIRST GRAND PRIX • BRAZIL, 1978

GRANDS PRIX CONTESTED • 271

WINS • 0

At the first race of the 1996 season in Australia the Arrows team could not afford to buy any chairs. They ate their lunch sitting on the concrete floor of the garage. On either side, rivals used cheap and cheerful garden furniture to seat guests and team members on the grass lawn running the length of the garage block. It summed up Arrows Grand Prix International, a team which has continually failed to find a place in the sun.

The team from Milton Keynes could not claim a shortage of either time or experience. With more than 270 Grand Prix starts to their credit, Arrows hold the unenviable record of running the longest without a win. It is a tribute to the management's resilience that the team have managed to survive with a CV showing just one pole position and a handful of second places as the high point of an involvement stretching across more than eighteen seasons.

The future looked bright following a takeover by the TWR Group early in 1996. There have been mergers and buyouts before – so many that at times it has been difficult to know precisely how the team should be named – but the wholesale shake-up by Tom Walkinshaw Racing promises to drill much-needed life and funding into a team which otherwise seemed destined to be professional also-rans.

Such a harsh summary would be an unfair reflection on the unstinting efforts of one man, without whom Arrows would have collapsed long ago. Jackie Oliver is a founding member of the team and his place within motor racing cannot be understated. A former Grand Prix driver, Oliver is central to the Arrows story and much that went on before the birth of the team in 1978.

Born in Romford in 1943, Oliver was a typical cocky Essex lad who qualified as a heating and ventilation engineer. He arrived on the racing scene at the age of seventeen, racing a Mini in club events before moving on to sports cars and single-seaters. Originally the racing had been no more than a hobby, but the move up the ladder threatened to take him away from the family commercial refrigeration business and led to a temporary internal rift. He pursued his ambition and it was indicative of natural persuasive powers that he won motor sport sponsorship from a flying club, his Formula Two Lotus showing signs of support from the Herts and Essex Aero Club in 1968. That season, spent mainly in Europe, included a race at Hockenheim in Germany and it was there on 7 April that a dreadful event had a far-reaching effect on Oliver's future.

The world of motor sport was devastated when Jim Clark, a seemingly indestructible genius, was killed after his Formula Two Lotus crashed into a tree. Apart from anything else, it left a vacancy in the Lotus Grand Prix team and Oliver was selected for the impossible task of replacing the former World Champion.

ARROWS

◄◄ Page 8:
*Ricardo Rosset (right)
and Arrows: ready
to improve*

**Arrows hold the
unenviable record of
running the longest
without a win**

▲ Arrows: the quiet
end of the pit lane.
For the moment

Clark and Colin Chapman, the founder and the guiding light of Lotus, had a rapport which bordered on a father and son relationship. Anyone else was bound to fall short in Chapman's esteem, particularly if they did not possess Clark's gentle, retiring nature. Oliver started off on the wrong foot at Monaco, where he crashed on the opening lap of his first Grand Prix, Chapman having specifically instructed his young protégé not to do anything stupid. Oliver found himself unemployed the minute he met up with his boss, but Chapman relented and Oliver showed his gratitude by finishing fifth in the next race in Belgium.

One way or another, it was quite a dramatic season, particularly on the fast road circuit at Rouen, where Oliver had a massive accident during practice for the French Grand Prix. The reason for the 140 m.p.h. crash was never clear but the end result saw the rear wheels and gearbox flung thirty yards from the rest of the car once the wreckage

ARROWS   11

ARROWS

had finally come to a halt. Showing no ill effects from such a terrifying shunt, Oliver went to his home Grand Prix at Brands Hatch and led confidently until the transmission broke. Had he actually won, his driving career would have followed a different direction: he never led a Grand Prix again and found himself without a contract at the end of the year.

A third-place finish in the final race of the season had at least ensured his reputation was good enough to secure a drive with BRM, an association which would last for two years with very little reward. Oliver then switched full time to sports car racing in 1971, his travels taking him to North America and the CanAm series. It was there that he met Don Nichols, an entrepreneur who, one way or another, played a major role in his career over the next decade.

Nichols owned Shadow Cars, and when he decided to expand beyond CanAm and build a Grand Prix car Oliver was the natural choice to drive it. It took some time for the Formula One operation to gel, and at the end of their first season in 1973 Oliver chose to race in North America while continuing to work with the Shadow Formula One operation. He raced in the occasional Grand Prix, his last being in Sweden in 1977, by which time he was heavily involved in the operational side of the business.

◀ *The power behind Arrows: Brian Hart, the engine guru, and Jackie Oliver (right)*

Oliver and Alan Rees (the team manager at Shadow) were increasingly at odds with the policy preferred by Nichols and plans were secretly laid to set up their own team in 1978. Tony Southgate and Dave Wass (the designer and the draughtsman at Shadow) threw in their lot. The new team would be known as Arrows. The letters AR stood for the Italian sponsor, Franco Ambrosio, R for Rees, O for Oliver, W for Wass and S for Southgate. On 28 November 1977, the team moved into a new factory in Milton Keynes.

The most pressing problem was to have a new car designed and built in time for the start of the season. The first race, scheduled for 15 January in Argentina, was out of the question but they simply had to be ready for the Brazilian Grand Prix two weeks later. Since the team were anxious to become members of the Formula One Constructors' Association (FOCA) and enjoy the benefits which came with that, they had to comply with the rules which demanded that they could miss just one non-European race. It was a tall order but, in the space of sixty days, the new car was ready.

Such was the urgency that the press launch carried on as planned despite the Silverstone pit lane and track being covered with snow. The car was then air-freighted to Rio de Janeiro in time for Riccardo Patrese to qualify respectably and finish the sixty-three-lap race tenth, but by no means last. It was a miraculous achievement. Oliver and his boys would pay the price in a courtroom a few months later.

In the meantime, Arrows became the talk of the paddock at the next race, in South Africa. Patrese qualified in seventh place, and as if to prove this had not been a one-lap wonder, the Italian sat comfortably with the leaders, gradually moving forward, until on lap twenty-one he was in second place. Then, calm as you like, five laps later the white and gold Arrows moved into the lead and began to pull away. The Formula One regulars could not believe what they were seeing. A new team, a brand-new car, and a driver in only his eleventh Grand Prix (Patrese having made his Formula One debut with Shadow the previous season). It was too good to be true.

On the sixty-fourth lap, with fourteen to go, the Ford engine blew up. The Arrows rolled to the side of the track and a disconsolate Patrese climbed out. By the time he reached the pits he was in tears. He said there had been no warning whatsoever. A fairy tale win had been there for the asking. It would take him four more years to score his maiden win. Arrows would wish they could be that lucky.

Patrese collected the first world championship point for Arrows by finishing sixth in the next race, at Long Beach in California, a result he repeated at Monaco a few weeks later. The season continued with an excellent second place in Sweden in June but questions were being asked about how it had been possible to design and build a new car from scratch in such a short time. The heaviest doubts were coming from the direction of Shadow, where Don Nichols was claiming that the Arrows was, in fact, a copy of the 1978 Shadow which Southgate had designed before leaving (and which had not been completed until after the Arrows had appeared). To prove his point, Nichols decided to take Arrows to court in London.

It turned out to be an unpleasant legal tussle, complicated slightly by the fact that Mr Ambrosio had been thrown into jail for offences unrelated to the racing team. *Motoring News*, reporting the case on 27 July 1978, said that Oliver had explained to the High Court judge why he had split from Shadow. Oliver said he had thought his former employers were heading for financial collapse and not all of the sponsorship money was being used on Formula One development. He claimed he was owed money by Shadow. He also said Southgate had held discussions with a solicitor over use of the drawings and it had been decided those drawings could be used.

In evidence, Nichols said Oliver had sought to make heroes of Arrows and had campaigned to discredit the Shadow team, and claimed that he had been left with an almost empty factory and no staff. Had it not been for the loyalty of his sponsor, he would have been unable continue.

After a lengthy hearing, Mr Justice Templeman found in Nichols's favour and declared that it was not possible for Arrows to have produced a car so quickly without the use of copies of some Shadow drawings. He declared 40 per cent of the components had been so copied and banned the car from racing.

Southgate, perhaps sensing defeat, had already begun a new car in early June and it had been completed in less time than the original Arrows. The car was ready for the Austrian Grand Prix on 13 August, thus ensuring Arrows had not missed a race. That would be the only good news in a difficult second half of the season. Patrese was involved, directly and indirectly, in collisions at the start of the next three races, the latter at Monza having far-reaching consequences.

The start of the Italian Grand Prix had always been a fairly haphazard affair given the tension which pulsates through the Monza autodrome on a warm September afternoon. The race in 1978 was no exception, an anxious starter unleashing the field before Patrese, delayed at the beginning of the final parade lap, had reached his grid position. Patrese floored the throttle and made full use of the wide start–finish straight before it narrowed viciously into a tight bottleneck. In the inevitable chaos, several cars collided, including the Lotus of Ronnie Peterson. The Swedish driver was removed to hospital, where he died later that evening.

Patrese was blamed. James Hunt, running alongside Peterson, said the Arrows had forced him into the Lotus. Pictures published in the Italian magazine *Autosprint*

Nichols decided to take Arrows to court in London

 ARROWS

▲ **Arrows have been gambling without success since 1978**

proved categorically that when Patrese joined the main stream of traffic moments before arriving at the bottleneck the Arrows had already overtaken Hunt. Nonetheless, Patrese's aggressive driving in previous races had been the subject of complaint and the drivers were out to teach him a lesson. In an unprecedented move, they successfully sought to have him banned from the next race, in the United States, even though he was entirely innocent in this instance. It was a knee-jerk reaction which was to shame most of the drivers concerned when they thought about it some time later in less emotional circumstances.

For Arrows, the Monza affair was further aggravation they did not need. Nonetheless, their first year of operation had netted eleven championship points and somehow they had survived the embarrassment of the High Court scandal the previous July.

The year had taken its toll in many respects, not least the realization that Arrows could not become members of FOCA after all, thanks to the finding of the court case with

Shadow. In effect, the ruling said that an Arrows did not exist until Southgate's second car had been built for the Austrian Grand Prix. In FOCA's terms, therefore, an Arrows had not completed the required number of races. The rush to make ready for Brazil seven months before had largely been a wasted effort and exclusion from FOCA meant the absence of travel subsidies worth £50,000.

In an effort to catch their breath and save money, Arrows decided to develop their existing car for 1979. Two races into the season, mediocre placings meant there was no alternative but to build a new car after all. It was not ready until July. It was hardly worth waiting for.

The Arrows A2 was a disaster from the moment it first turned a wheel, an adventurous bullet nose and angled position for the engine and gearbox upsetting the handling to a disastrous degree. In the end, the team had to resort to revised versions of the old car for drivers Patrese and Jochen Mass. They managed just five championship points between them during a very disappointing year.

1980 was not much better, a brand-new car failing to meet the demands of the latest aerodynamic developments mastered by the leading teams. Arrows not only lost Tony Southgate but also their long-standing sponsor, Warsteiner. Money had been tight before; now it was almost non-existent and the workforce was put on short time during the winter.

Oliver set to work and found support from two Italian companies. Dave Wass, meanwhile, assumed responsibility for modifying the car to meet new regulations which would reduce the aerodynamic effects Arrows had failed to capitalize on in the first place. With a much simpler car, and everyone running on the same Michelin tyres following the withdrawal of Goodyear, Arrows were suddenly on the pace, so much so that Patrese stunned everyone by claiming pole position for the Long Beach Grand Prix. He led the race until the fuel pressure faltered. He followed that up with third place in Brazil and a second at Imola. The team was on a roll. It was too good to last.

When Goodyear returned halfway through the season to service a handful of the top teams, Michelin panicked. In a bid to answer the challenge, the French firm concentrated on their leading runners – and dropped Arrows. For the rest of the season Oliver's team ran with Pirelli; the Italian tyres were no match for the best their rivals could offer, and Arrows never really recovered. The struggle continued through 1982. A Goodyear contract was arranged for the following year, but having sorted out their tyres Arrows were now being left behind by the development of turbocharged engines. It was no surprise to learn that they could not afford one.

The team were now in severe financial problems but relief seemed at hand when Oliver persuaded British American Tobacco to support his team as a means of launching their low-nicotine Barclay cigarettes. A last-minute deal was arranged for the use of a BMW turbo but the engine was an off-the-shelf customer version, less powerful than the works turbos being supplied to Brabham though powerful enough to cause problems for a chassis designer unaccustomed to the jump in performance. By 1985, Team Barclay Arrows had begun to sort themselves out, Thierry Boutsen and Gerhard Berger – two young drivers using Arrows as the first step on the Formula One ladder – earning fourteen points, the team's highest score since its inception.

BAT made way for an American finance company, USF&G, and in 1988 the team seemed to be making a modicum of progress by finishing fourth in the Constructors' Championship. And yet, and yet. In the background there remained a lingering doubt which was best summed up by Doug Nye in his review of the 1988 season in the authoritative annual *Autocourse*.

'Arrows remain something of an enigma,' wrote Nye. 'Most teams are either progressing or declining, but for years Arrows have remained consistently at the same level. A hefty nudge, one feels, could at last set them moving, but which way may depend on the nature of the nudge . . . '

The answer seemed to be 'in a positive direction' when in October 1989 a liaison was formed with the Footwork Corporation; the Japanese conglomerate became a major shareholder and corporate sponsor of the team, now known as Footwork Arrows. The next important phase in the redevelopment programme was revealed four months later when a three-year deal was struck with Porsche for the supply of engines built

The team were now in severe financial problems

specifically for Arrows by this prestigious company. Finally, it seemed, the team's ambitions would be realized. This was the nudge in the right direction. In fact, it would turn out to be an even bigger disaster than those which had gone before.

Porsche, absent from Formula One since they ran a turbocharged engine with McLaren in 1987, seriously underestimated the technical progress that had been made in Grand Prix racing. Perhaps still flushed with the success of their operation with McLaren, they showed an amazing mixture of arrogance and ignorance by producing a twelve-cylinder engine which was grossly overweight and underpowered. Fundamental problems with the oil pressure meant the cars could run for no more than two laps without an engine failure.

It was an unmitigated fiasco. The Footwork Corporation had reputedly invested $35 million in the engine and Arrows had expanded their workforce to 160 people. There was no alternative but to ditch the Porsche mid-season and switch to a proprietary Ford-Cosworth V8 as a stopgap measure. Not surprisingly, Footwork Arrows failed to score a single point in 1991. By November, an arrangement had been made for the team to use Mugen-prepared Honda engines in 1992.

The sole aim was to pull themselves out of the mire. The shambles of 1991 had reduced Footwork Arrows to the bottom of the league table and into the role of pre-qualifying, an undignified scramble among the lesser teams for the right to go forward and take part in official practice and qualifying. The car, designed by Alan Jenkins, was uncomplicated, and the engine reliable. Thanks to the efforts of Michele Alboreto, an experienced and competent driver who had enjoyed the peak of his career with Ferrari, the team rebuilt their reputation sufficiently to allow a more adventurous car for 1993. Unfortunately, Footwork and Arrows were left behind once again in the technology race and just two finishes in the points raised questions about the viability of the relationship between them, particularly in the light of a biting recession in Japan.

Wataru Ohashi, chairman of the Footwork Corporation, responded by retaining the ownership of Arrows but reducing his company's involvement, and the team was entered for the 1994 season as Arrows Grand Prix International. In other words, the funding would indeed be reduced and the Arrows saga would therefore continue through the next two seasons. A change of engine supply from the customer Ford V8 in 1994 to the neat and potentially excellent Hart V8 in 1995 would be compromised by the lack of finance. At no stage could Footwork Arrows struggle above eighth place in the Constructors' Championship. It had become a depressingly familiar story.

Matters seemed even worse in 1996 when team members did not have seats to sit on at the opening race in Melbourne. There was talk of Hart refusing to supply engines if

There was no alternative but to ditch the Porsche mid-season

bills were not paid. The team was ripe for purchase and a suitable buyer was not far away. In fact, he was in the garage next door.

Tom Walkinshaw had established a reputation for entrepreneurial skills which had seen him engineer the winning Jaguars at Le Mans and mastermind the technical changes which made Benetton a championship team. A more recent brief had been the reshaping of Ligier. When Walkinshaw's plans to buy the French team were frustrated by the owner's intransigence, his attention was drawn to the financial plight of Arrows.

A deal was struck almost immediately. Tom Walkinshaw Racing (TWR) became the new owners of Arrows Grand Prix International. Jackie Oliver and Alan Rees would run the team, but Walkinshaw would call the important shots. Given the Scotsman's no-nonsense style, it seemed that Arrows might at long last complete the slow trip from Shadow to sunshine.

BENETTON

BENETTON

BENETTON

DRIVERS:

JEAN ALESI (FRANCE)

GERHARD BERGER (AUSTRIA)

TEAM PRINCIPAL • FLAVIO BRIATORE

CHIEF DESIGNER • ROSS BRAWN

CAR • BENETTON B196

ENGINE • RENAULT V10

FIRST GRAND PRIX (under Toleman name) • ITALY, 1981

GRANDS PRIX CONTESTED • 218

WINS • 26

At Benetton you hear the loudest music, see the brightest colours. The team director wears his cap back to front; he breaks every rule in the established etiquette of Formula One. It is a team which wants to be noticed, the sporting arm of a fashion company which likes to shock. Models drape themselves across the racing cars; members of the media, pariahs elsewhere in the pit lane, are made conspicuously welcome. Benetton is chic, racy, ambitious. It is also successful. But what makes the prosperity acceptable is the fact that Benetton came from nowhere in a remarkably short time. Two world championships in succession were achieved through graft rather than inherited through money. It is a familiar theme within the Benetton organization as a whole.

◀◀ Page 24:
A team full of character. Flavio Briatore (right) in heavy discussion with Gerhard Berger

The glossy literature speaks of how Luciano Benetton used to travel around his home town in northern Italy on a bicycle, delivering his sister's hand-knitted sweaters to customers. Twenty-five years later, in 1987, the cottage industry had grown to a multi-national group worth millions. There were more than 4,000 Benetton outlets in sixty countries. On average, two new franchises were opening every day. And the company ran its own Grand Prix team, Benetton Formula.

Motor sport at its highest level provided the desired image of excitement and style for a successful designer label. The two were made for each other. The irony was that the struggling Formula One team which Benetton had bought at the end of 1985 had come from deepest Essex and the grimy world of lorries and diesel fumes. The Toleman team was hardly high fashion. But then Benetton was scarcely Ferrari. It was a marriage of sporting convenience.

The Toleman team was hardly high fashion

The only link between Toleman and Luciano Benetton's early activities was the delivery of goods. The Toleman Group was formed in 1926 to transport new and used cars, the business flourishing in fifty years to embrace a fleet of 500 vehicles to shift 600,000 new motor cars each year to dealers in the UK.

The company chairman, Albert Toleman, went rallying in his spare time, but the firm did not become involved in racing until Alex Hawkridge, a director of Toleman, agreed to support a friend's efforts with a saloon car in British club racing. When that project lost its momentum Hawkridge and Bob Toleman, the younger of Albert Toleman's two sons, enrolled with a racing drivers' school and, suitably enthused, went on to buy a Formula Ford each for the 1976 season. Hawkridge in particular proved adept but enthusiasm for the sport within the Toleman Group received a massive setback when Bob crashed, and died from his injuries.

Involvement tended to be low-key from there on, Bob's elder brother Ted dabbling now and again on the racetrack while Hawkridge channelled the company's support

*▲ Ahead of the old firm.
Jean Alesi keeps a
Ferrari at bay*

towards Rad Dougall, a young South African. Dougall's promise was fulfilled when he won two major Formula Ford championships in 1977, and Hawkridge was so enthusiastic that he hoisted him straight past Formula Three and into the international scene by providing the funding for a Formula Two car. Talk of the Toleman-backed team learning the ropes in 1978, winning races the following year and the championship the next was considered a touch optimistic. In fact, it turned out to be a cautious prediction.

Dougall did struggle during the first year, and even more so in 1979, but the team had expanded into a two-car operation, the second driver, Brian Henton, coming close to winning the title. It was evident however that Toleman would not be in full control of their destiny for as long as they had to rely on buying cars and engines from companies such as March and BMW, who were committed to running their own teams. Hawkridge took the bull by the horns in 1980 and decided that the only way to succeed would be

◄ *Berger: team driver in 1996*

for Toleman to do everything themselves. Henton and a cocky Hampshire lad by the name of Derek Warwick would do the driving. Power would come from engines built by Brian Hart, a talented privateer based in Harlow. Financial support would be provided by BP.

The Toleman-Harts ran riot. The immaculately presented yellow, white and green cars were quick and reliable, Henton taking the title he had narrowly missed in 1979. On the wave of this outstanding success, Toleman Group Motorsport, as the team was known, confidently announced that they would move up to Grand Prix racing. They were in for a very rude awakening.

The understandable enthusiasm for the project tended to gloss over the fact that Toleman's experience as chassis builders was strictly limited; Brian Hart had never constructed a turbocharged engine before; the team's tyre supplier, Pirelli, would be new to Formula One; and neither driver had any experience of Grand Prix racing. On top of that, they joined at a time when Formula One was being torn in two by a political war over who controlled the sport. Otherwise, Toleman's entry was pretty straightforward . . .

Despite having received dispensation to miss the opening races of the 1981 season in faraway places such as Brazil and Argentina, it was a push to be ready for the first race in Europe, the San Marino Grand Prix at Imola. You could tell that the team sensed trouble when a press release, issued a few days before the team's debut, was headed *Outlining the problems facing the Toleman Team at Imola*. It did not make optimistic reading. And rightly so. The new car, a bulky device known as the TG181, was as slow as it looked. Neither driver qualified for the race.

Reflecting some time later on the team's first effort, Rory Byrne, the designer of the TG181, said that new car was outdated within a month of its first appearance. Some would have said it was not as good as that.

Henton and Warwick struggled manfully with the unwieldy car, known at first as the Flying Pig and then dubbed the Belgrano, a tongue-in-cheek reference to the elderly Argentinian battleship which had been sunk during the Falklands War. After a frustrating summer of endless problems and non-qualifications, Henton managed to heave the TG181 onto the grid for the Italian Grand Prix at Monza. When the team repaired to their hotel that night it was as though they had won the race. Henton went on to finish a distant tenth; hardly a front-line performance, but at least the car and engine were reliable. Warwick made his Formula One debut at the final race in Las Vegas, making it just two starts for the team in the season. Toleman knew they had to begin somewhere. But they had never imagined it would be as difficult as this.

For 1982, Henton made way for Teo Fabi. The Italian may have been keen to break into Grand Prix racing but he must have wondered about the wisdom of the decision as he wrestled with the unloved TG181 and failed to qualify for the first three races. Warwick was beginning to make progress by qualifying now and again but the team found much-needed breathing space when their transporter broke down on the way home from Monaco, a handy get-out from the long-haul trip to Detroit and Montreal. With the benefit of time to go testing, Warwick qualified in thirteenth place for the Dutch Grand Prix. He retired with a broken oil pipe but the mood was upbeat for the team's home event at Brands Hatch.

Both cars qualified on the eighth row and Warwick caused a considerable stir when he urged the big car through the field, picking rivals off one by one and moving into a remarkable third place. It was difficult to believe when the Belgrano then outbraked a Ferrari into Paddock Bend at the end of the pit straight. A Toleman – second! The place went berserk. Then a collective groan a few laps later as Warwick coasted to a halt. The official reason given was broken transmission. There are those who believe to this day that the Toleman was running with little fuel on board and the turbo set at maximum boost. No matter. The headlines had been made, ALAS – POOR WARWICK being the most inventive.

The new car, a bulky device known as the TG181, was as slow as it looked

Despite that flash of promise, Toleman finished the 1982 season no further on than they had been at the start. Fabi had failed to finish a single race; Warwick had made it to the flag just twice, his best result tenth in Germany. It was high time for a new car.

The TG183, unveiled in August, had proved fast straight away but had then given trouble in its two race appearances. Nonetheless, Rory Byrne had a decent basis to work on – until the sport's governing body changed the technical regulations overnight. They said the rule changes would affect each team equally. That may have been the way it looked on paper, but it really hurt a small team struggling to survive.

Toleman had received support from Candy Domestic Appliances in 1981, but the Italian company then took their money elsewhere, leaving Toleman to find the majority of backing from within the group during 1982. It was essential that the new car – now known as the TG183B in its latest guise – should show promise. Toleman went off to Brazil for winter testing. The lap times were immediately impressive and Candy came back on board for 1983 with the proviso that two cars be entered for every race, the second to be driven by the Italian Bruno Giacomelli.

Warwick kicked off the season with eighth place in Brazil. Then followed a series of retirements due to accidents, most notably at Monaco where Warwick, gambling by starting with slick tyres on a wet but drying track, had worked his way into third place before colliding with the car in front. Despite the failures to finish, the positive aspect was that both cars were qualifying regularly. If only the car and engine would hold together and the drivers remained on the track, championship points might be there for the asking.

The great moment came in Holland, where Warwick finished an excellent fourth. It had taken thirty-eight races, but judging by the unconfined joy in the Toleman camp the wait had been worth it. And once he had a taste, Warwick collected points in the remaining three races. It was enough to persuade Renault to make the Englishman an offer for 1984. While everyone at Toleman was extremely sad to lose the man who had been such an integral part of the team, his departure turned out to be fortunate. Alex Hawkridge filled the vacancy with Ayrton Senna.

The Brazilian had just won the British Formula Three Championship and several team managers had noted his promise. Senna had received offers from the likes of McLaren but he wisely chose to make a low-key entry to Formula One with a team in which the pressure would not be so great. Such was his confidence that he knew his day would come. In the meantime, Toleman would be the perfect place.

Senna accepted that he would have to persevere with the TG183B for the first few races at least, but the expression took on a more acute meaning during the second round of the championship in South Africa. Debris on the track struck the front of the

The great moment came in Holland, where Warwick finished an excellent fourth

▲ *Gerhard Berger,*
the tallest driver in
Formula One, sits low
in the cockpit of the
Benetton-Renault

Toleman and removed the upper deck of the broad wing which contained the water radiators and stretched across the breadth of the car. The resulting loss of aerodynamic aid made the steering heavy and the car difficult to drive. He held sixth place, but not satisfied with that he pressed on in the hope that he might snatch fifth on the final lap. Despite being close to exhaustion, he set his fastest lap of the race and had to be satisfied with sixth place.

The effort had taken his mind off the discomfort. When he took the flag and dropped his hands from the steering wheel for the first time in ninety minutes, Senna suddenly found his arms were leaden. He could barely regain control of the car and had to be helped from the cockpit once he had managed to come to a halt. The Toleman team were not alone in being highly impressed.

Senna, however, was distinctly unimpressed two races later when Toleman became

◀ **His Benetton abandoned, Jean Alesi sprints back to the pits for the back-up car**

embroiled in a financial dispute with Pirelli, the team's tyre supplier. The net result was no running for Senna on the first day of practice and then a blown engine on the second day, which meant a failure to qualify for the San Marino Grand Prix. Senna was not amused, particularly when his team-mate for 1984, Johnny Cecotto, had made it onto the grid.

Toleman ran Michelin tyres from then on and, enhancing their performance further, Rory Byrne had produced a neat new car. Senna was poised to make full use of the combination during a dramatic race at Monaco. Rain, the great equalizer in motor racing, put every driver on the same slippery footing. Senna passed leading lights such as Rosberg and Lauda as if they were standing still. After nineteen laps, with sixty to go, he was in second place and closing on the leader, Alain Prost. It was a consummate display of artistry and confidence in such perilous conditions.

Unfortunately, in the opinion of the clerk of the course – who happened to be an experienced racing driver – the danger went beyond an acceptable level when the rain intensified. The race was brought to a premature end. Senna had closed to within seven seconds of Prost and there was outrage in the Toleman pit. The chance of a wonderful victory had been taken from them. No matter that the third-place car, a Tyrrell, was going even faster than Senna. A point had been made. Toleman was well and truly established.

Senna's embryonic genius brought the team third places in Britain and at the last race of the season in Portugal, by which time he had been lured to Lotus. As things would turn out, he was leaving in the nick of time. Toleman was about to enter a period of serious disarray.

A new car had been designed for 1985. Unfortunately, there would be no tyres on which to run it. Michelin had pulled out of Formula One, leaving Toleman in a quandary. Goodyear's allocation was already accounted for and Pirelli, following the acrimonious parting of ways with Toleman the previous May, was not about to fill the breach. As a result, the team remained idle during the first three races.

Toleman was about to enter a period of serious disarray

A solution was found by buying out the Pirelli supply allocated to a small team which was on the point of closure. And, significantly, the deal was put together thanks to considerable financial support from Benetton.

This was the clothing company's third season in Formula One, the first having been spent as sponsors of the Tyrrell team before adopting a similar role with Alfa Romeo in 1984. The link with the Italian team remained throughout 1985 but it soon became clear that Benetton had more serious intentions than acting as sponsor. The Toleman was painted white and carried the soon to be familiar symbol 'The United Colors of Benetton' across every surface. The period of inactivity had set back the team's development programme and it took Rory Byrne and his engineers most of the summer to haul their single entry towards the front of the grid.

At the Nürburgring in August, Teo Fabi shook the establishment by putting the Toleman on pole position for the German Grand Prix. He retired from that race – as he would from all bar one of the Grands Prix entered by Toleman – but the team's potential was enough to encourage Benetton to go the whole hog and become an entrant. The timing was right. A bid for was accepted. From now on, the team would be known as Benetton Formula. Toleman Group Motorsport was no more.

Part of the deal included a switch from the trusty Hart engine to the well-heeled efforts of BMW and their four-cylinder turbo. The late change made Byrne's life just as difficult as before as he attempted to produce a new car in a matter of months, added to

BENETTON

which was the complication of making the chassis long enough to accommodate Gerhard Berger, the lanky Austrian joining Fabi on the driving strength. It was obviously going to take time for the new combination to find its feet and there were no decent results forthcoming until mid-season. Then the Benetton-BMWs took off.

At the super-fast Osterreichring Fabi claimed pole position with Berger alongside on the front row. The green and white cars with the colourful markings shot off the line, the explosive power of the BMW turbos carrying them into a race of their own. Then Fabi over-revved his engine and Berger suffered a niggling failure within the tiny on-board battery. Fabi was on pole again in Italy, a puncture causing his demise on this occasion. But in Mexico, Berger never ran lower than fourth and was perfectly positioned to make the most of the durability of his Pirelli tyres. While his Goodyear-shod rivals were forced to change tyres, Berger ran non-stop to give Benetton their first Grand Prix victory.

Peter Collins, the team manager, then faced the dilemma of deciding which national anthem should be played in honour of the team: the Italian, in deference to the owners, or the British to signify a car built in Britain? Turning to the team patron, Luciano Benetton, Collins received an immediate answer. 'God save the Queen' rang out over the victory rostrum. Benetton would not be placed in such a pleasant predicament for some considerable time.

Rory Byrne faced a frantic off-season when Benetton decided to change engines yet again, this time switching from BMW to a Ford turbo V6. Berger was replaced by Thierry Boutsen, who combined with Fabi to give the team eleven top six finishes and fifth place in the Constructors' Championship. The tireless Byrne was sent back to his drawing board when yet another change of engine was deemed necessary for 1988, the Ford turbo giving way to a normally aspirated V8 from the same manufacturer. This would be the last year of the turbocharged engine and it had been hoped that restrictions on the turbos would favour the V8. That turned out to be far from the case, although commendable consistency by Boutsen and his new team-mate, Alessandro Nannini, helped Benetton take third place in the constructors' series.

That was all very well but somehow the team lacked the impetus to take them onto the same level as pace-setters such as McLaren and Ferrari. Benetton had gone as far as they could – but did not appear to know what to do next. 1989 marked the beginning of a major change. Luciano Benetton called in Flavio Briatore.

The appointment was ridiculed by the Formula One cognoscenti. Who was this man? What did he know about Grand Prix racing? Briatore was the first to admit that he knew nothing at all. In fact, he saw that supposed shortcoming as a major advantage. There would be no preconceived ideas. Briatore's would be a fresh approach.

◄◄ *Benetton finished second in the 1996 Brazilian Grand Prix*

1989 marked the beginning of a major change

BENETTON

▲ A typical story at the start of 1996: Jean Alesi parked by the side of the track

Born in Turin in 1950, Briatore became an insurance salesman after leaving school and then moved into the stockbroking business, where he met Luciano Benetton in 1974. Seven years later, he was in America, establishing Benetton's name on behalf of the family. Having gained Benetton's trust and made a success of the American division, he was Luciano's first choice when it came to grabbing the Formula One team by the throat and lifting it onto the highest level.

Benetton did not want to know about employing someone with Formula One experience. The decision came as no surprise to Briatore, who had once seen Luciano take a liking to a waiter in a Los Angeles restaurant. The next day the waiter was managing a Benetton shop. It was typical of Benetton's knack of operating by intuition. First, though, Briatore would have to go to the races with the team in 1989 and simply observe a world which was completely alien. The racing itself held some attraction, the technical side absolutely none. It was the commercial opportunities – largely unexploited by those for whom racing came first – which intrigued Briatore the most.

Briatore began to ask questions which seemed naive. Why, he wanted to know, could one of the team's drivers not walk properly? Briatore was referring to Johnny Herbert, a young Englishman whose rapid and brilliant climb to the top had received a major

set-back during a Formula 3000 race the previous August. Herbert had been involved in a crash which seriously injured his feet and ankles. But showing fine sporting form, Peter Collins had stood by an earlier decision to give Herbert his chance with Benetton in Formula One.

Herbert worked excruciatingly hard on his fitness over the winter and made a sensational debut by finishing fourth in his first Grand Prix. Thereafter, however, the legacy of the injuries hampered his performances. Herbert could barely walk when out of the car and, while his innate sense of balance and speed remained, the inability to stamp hard on the brake pedal was reflected in his lap times. Collins remained commendably loyal throughout.

Briatore suggested that this was no way to win races. The absence of sentiment offended many. But looked at from Briatore's impartial and practical stance, the logic was obvious. Herbert was 'rested' halfway through the season. Briatore took over the commercial activities as managing director the following August. Collins left the team soon after.

▲ Renault powered Benetton to the World Championship in 1995. The betting was that the combination could not repeat the result in 1996

38   **BENETTON**

Briatore, with the considerable advantage of an open chequebook, lured John Barnard, one of the most sought-after designers in Formula One. Then he made a curious decision; he signed Nelson Piquet, a three-times World Champion who was perceived to have passed his best.

Piquet joined Alessandro Nannini, a star of the future who had lucked into Benetton's second win the previous October after Senna and McLaren had been disqualified from the 1989 Japanese Grand Prix. Briatore had done his homework. He had discovered that Piquet was indolent and motivated by money. Briatore said he would pay the Brazilian on performance. It was the first time such a thing had been done to a top driver in Formula One, Piquet having been more accustomed to collecting a seven-figure sum regardless of how he performed. Briatore agreed to pay $100,000 for every championship point scored by Piquet. At the end of the 1990 season, Piquet had earned $4.3 million thanks to a consistent run and two victories. No one thought he had it in him. Benetton's bank balance may have been reduced, but Briatore's stock had risen.

The first of the two wins had come in Japan, Piquet leading a Benetton one-two. The second car, however, was not driven by Nannini; the likeable Italian's promising Formula One career had come to a shocking end a few weeks before when his right arm had been severed in a helicopter accident. Although the limb was reattached by the marvels of surgery, his future in motor sport would be restricted to racing saloon cars.

Nannini's place had been taken by Roberto Moreno, and on the strength of that second place in Japan – his best result by far in an otherwise undistinguished career – the Brazilian was given a permanent seat at Benetton alongside Piquet for 1991. Moreno managed a few finishes in the points but his generally lack-lustre performances left him wide open for rough treatment in the wake of Briatore's next controversial move.

It was in August 1991 that Michael Schumacher first appeared on the Formula One scene. The young German driver had previously driven sports cars for Mercedes-Benz but no one in Formula One had taken much notice; no one except Eddie Jordan. The astute Irishman, on finding he had a vacancy to fill thanks to the incarceration of one his drivers following an unfortunate incident with a London cabbie, gave Schumacher his chance. The novice was sensational and claimed seventh place on the grid for the Belgian Grand Prix. Jordan thought he had it made. He reckoned without Briatore.

Two weeks later in Italy, Schumacher was driving a Benetton, Moreno had been bundled onto the sidelines and Jordan was left holding the tattered remains of what he thought was a contract with his young star. As far as Briatore was concerned, it was good business, particularly when Schumacher went on to finish fifth in Italy.

Having found the driver around which to mould the future of the team, Briatore

Briatore said he would pay the Brazilian on performance

needed to sort out the technical department and make sure Schumacher had the equipment he deserved. Barnard had left the team mid-season. Briatore took on board Tom Walkinshaw, a self-made man with a genius for organizing racing teams.

Walkinshaw's brief, as director of engineering, was to knock Benetton Formula into shape and pull all the potentially excellent strands together. Walkinshaw brought along Ross Brawn, the designer who had engineered the Jaguars which had won Le Mans for Tom Walkinshaw Racing. Together they could see a major shortcoming in the Benetton set-up. It was literally all over the place.

At the time of the takeover in 1985, Benetton had acquired the Toleman premises on a trading estate in Witney in Oxfordshire. With room within the factory extremely limited, the team had expanded next door, and then to a unit across the road. John Barnard, on his arrival, had attempted to reorganize by purchasing new premises at Godalming in Surrey. The fact that they were a two-hour drive from Witney – but five minutes from Barnard's home – had not gone down well with the existing staff. Walkinshaw's first plan was to bring everything under one roof in Oxfordshire.

In the meantime, Benetton had to prepare as best they could for the 1992 season. Piquet had been dropped after winning only one race the previous year and being destroyed by Schumacher in the space of just five races. Martin Brundle was drafted into the team, the experienced Englishman – who had won the sports car world championship

◄ *In the hands of Michael Schumacher, a Benetton steering wheel could be made to work magic*

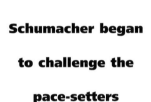

for Walkinshaw and Jaguar – making the ideal partner for the youngster. Schumacher proved devastatingly quick but Brundle, of all the drivers to work with the talented German, was to run him the closest.

The inevitable happened when Schumacher won his first Grand Prix in Belgium at the end of August, but Brundle had come close to victory, particularly in Canada where a mechanical failure had robbed him of maximum points. It had been Benetton's most competitive season yet. There were twenty-two finishes in the top six, each driver scoring points on eleven occasions to give Benetton third place in the Constructors' Championship.

In October 1992 the team moved to a purpose-built factory which had been merged skilfully into a hillside near the village of Enstone. The facilities were superb. They needed to be. Walkinshaw and his team had committed themselves to a massive programme of technical development which embraced everything from semi-automatic gearboxes to computer-controlled suspension. And just to complicate matters further, it was decided at the eleventh hour that it would be necessary to build a completely new car rather than rely on a development of the 1992 model. Talk about a challenge. It required commitment of the kind on which Briatore and the parent company thrived.

The first three races were disastrous, but as the season progressed the team got a handle on the potential of their car and Schumacher began to challenge the pace-setters, Williams-Renault. An impressive victory for Schumacher in Portugal contributed to Benetton finishing third in the Constructors' Championship, his team-mate Riccardo Patrese retiring from Formula One after being mercilessly worn down by Schumacher's brilliance and his willingness to adapt to the new technology.

Much of that sophisticated engineering was banned from Grand Prix racing for 1994 but Benetton's rush of success that year led cynics to believe that much of the trick equipment was still in use on their car. In a messy and unpleasant series of exchanges with the sport's governing body, nothing was proved when Benetton's equipment was examined. But the affair left a sour taste, both inside and outside the team.

The season had been billed as a head-to-head between Schumacher and Ayrton Senna but, sadly, it had come to a terrible and premature end when the Brazilian was killed during the third race of the season at Imola. Schumacher had won the first two and went on to claim four out of the next five before more controversy hit the team.

He was excluded from second place in the British Grand Prix and banned for two races after breaking the rules. His absence coincided with a rise to form by Damon Hill, and the two then waged a spectacular battle which lasted all the way to the final round of the championship in Australia. While disputing the lead on the streets of Adelaide the

Schumacher began to challenge the pace-setters

Benetton and the Williams collided. Michael Schumacher became World Champion on the spot.

It was an untidy end to a traumatic season which had also seen Benetton become embroiled in another debate, this time over the cause of a brief inferno while one of their cars was being refuelled during the German Grand Prix. At the end of the season, Benetton had been pipped by Williams for the Constructors' Championship. More than anything, Schumacher and the team wanted to set the record straight in 1995. However, they knew better than most that it would not be a simple matter.

The design office was thrown into a frenzy once more by a switch from the Ford V8 to the Renault V10, Briatore making the disruptive change simply because the French engine was the best. It took time for the team to find their feet, although Schumacher was fortunate to win the opening race of the season after Hill's Williams had retired with a mechanical failure. Hill won the next two races, and not only were Benetton struggling, but Schumacher made a rare mistake and crashed at Imola. It seemed as if Benetton had lost their way.

It was a clear sign of the team's strength in depth that they came back with a vengeance and took the fight to Williams. Sometimes it became over-intense, Schumacher and Hill colliding twice as they fought for the championship. On one occasion – at Silverstone – the second Benetton was there to take advantage, Johnny Herbert winning his first of two victories. The Englishman's return to the fold, albeit for just one season, proved that Briatore was a pragmatist after his dismissal of Herbert five years before.

There was no question about the best driver in 1995, Schumacher more or less wrapping up his second successive title with a brilliant drive at the Nürburgring in October. The celebrations would start in earnest after the penultimate round in Japan.

Brawn and Briatore arrived at Osaka's Kansai Airport at seven thirty on the Monday morning looking as through they had been up all night. Which they had – and with good reason. The day before, Schumacher had won the Japanese Grand Prix at Suzuka and, in so doing, he had handed the Constructors' Championship to Benetton as a follow-up to clinching the driver's title at Aida seven days previously. He had started from pole, led all the way, set fastest lap and, for good measure, his ninth win of the season equalled Nigel Mansell's record from 1992. It was a brilliant performance all round, one which was worthy of any champion.

Brawn and Briatore looked bemused, and in truth that had little to do with the alcoholic refreshment which had been flowing the night before. The fact was that Benetton had not started the season as favourites and yet here they were, the undisputed champions after blowing Williams away.

It seemed as if Benetton had lost their way

BENETTON

▲ Gerhard Berger: searching for points in the first half of 1996

Briatore, cap back-to-front as usual, denim shirt hanging out over his jeans, was in extremely good form, and much of his pleasure was derived from the upset his dishevelled appearance was causing among more dapper team owners as they made their way to the executive lounge. Every now and again Briatore, first-class boarding pass sticking out of his jacket pocket, would wander into the lounge with the mischievous intention of annoying his rivals some more.

The establishment, meanwhile, could not wait for 1996 in the belief that Briatore was about to get his come-uppance. Schumacher, the bedrock of the team, had been tempted by a $25 million offer from Ferrari, and Briatore had plumped for Jean Alesi and Gerhard Berger, drivers whose combined talent was not considered a match for Schumacher. Now we would know whether or not Benetton's success had been due to the driver or the team. Either way, Benetton would remain a vibrant part of the Formula One scene. The models would strut their stuff and the rock music would continue to play.

FERRARI

FERRARI

DRIVERS:

MICHAEL SCHUMACHER (GERMANY)

EDDIE IRVINE (IRELAND)

TEAM PRINCIPAL • LUCA DI MONTEZEMOLO

CHIEF DESIGNER • JOHN BARNARD

CAR • FERRARI F310

ENGINE • FERRARI V10

FIRST GRAND PRIX • ITALY, 1948

GRANDS PRIX CONTESTED • 554

WINS • 105

'Enzo Ferrari was a very clever and cunning old boy. For instance – and this is a silly little example – he would never be seen going for a pee. He actually said that to me: "Never go to the loo in public!" He didn't want anyone to see that he had to go for a pee; that he was just like the rest of us. He was very clever from that point of view. He worked very hard at creating his image and the myth of Ferrari. The "Old Man" really was something special. It was a privilege to have spent those years in Italy, to have been close to the throne, at it were, and to have seen the man who is a motoring legend.'

Dr Harvey Postlethwaite can speak with considerable authority. Currently the director of engineering with the Tyrrell team, he worked in Ferrari's Formula One design department between 1980 and 1988, followed by a two-year stint which ended in the autumn of 1993. By then, he had seen both ends of the spectrum. He had worked closely with Enzo Ferrari before the Old Man died on 14 August 1988, and he had returned to experience life at Ferrari under its parent company, Fiat. There was no comparison between the two regimes.

'Ferrari was a *super* team in the Eighties, when the Old Man was in charge,' he said. 'It was a *team*, and that spirit wasn't there when I returned. It never could be the same without Mr Ferrari.'

The death of Enzo Ferrari did indeed mark the end of an era. While the company has continued, the legend created by the ninety-year-old patriarch had finally come to a close. Ferrari is now controlled by Fiat's corporate reasoning rather than one man's emotions. And yet, such was the enormity of Enzo Ferrari's achievements, the mystical attraction generated by this giant of the automotive world lingers on.

Enzo Ferrari had been part and parcel of international motor racing since 1929 and yet it is hard to believe that he did not build his first Grand Prix car until he was forty-nine. Age did not matter to Enzo Ferrari any more than the increasing historical significance of the company which quickly matured in northern Italy, at Modena, and then in the nearby town of Maranello.

Ferrari was not interested in looking back at his achievements. Perhaps he knew it was unnecessary since no other team had come close to the nine world championships for drivers, eight constructors' titles, nine victories at Le Mans and eleven world sports car racing titles.

Ferraris have taken part in more than 550 Grands Prix since the start of the World Championship (of the current teams, only McLaren comes close with 440) and no Formula One race seems complete without at least one bright red Ferrari. Indeed, even

◀◀ Page 46:
As Ferrari team manager, Jean Todt took on the most difficult job in motor racing

Enzo Ferrari had been part and parcel of international motor racing since 1929

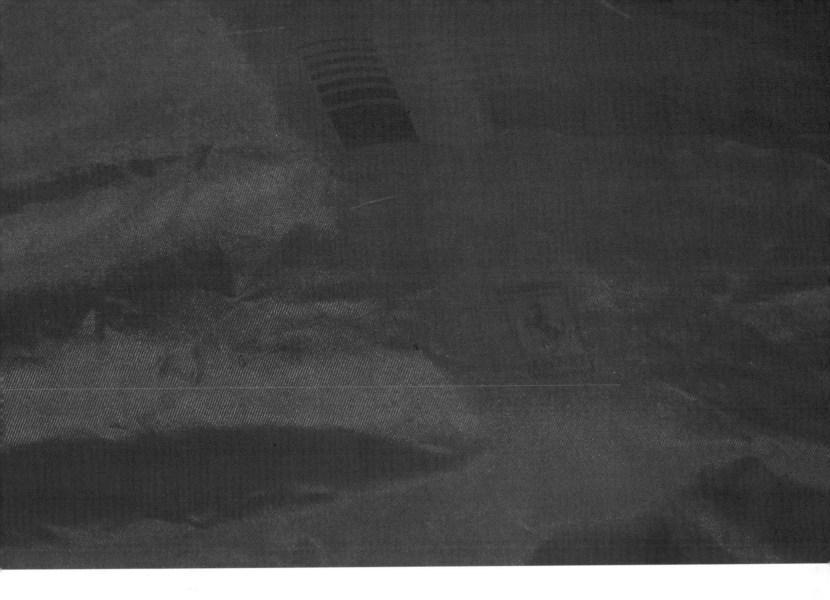

▲ Under cover but unmistakable: the black prancing horse, the symbol of a motor racing icon

though the team goes into decline at regular intervals, drivers continue to view a contract with Ferrari as the ultimate accolade. In Mr Ferrari's day, a nod of approval from the Old Man made the inevitable politicking seem almost bearable.

Enzo Ferrari knew the value of carefully orchestrated turmoil within the racing department and in his later years, although shaky on his feet, he retained a firm hand on the tiller of the team. The merger with Fiat in 1969 had allowed him to concentrate solely on his beloved racing (the road cars merely being an irritation, a means of providing finance for Enzo's motor racing aspirations) and it was only in the final months of his life that ill-health confined him to bed and allowed control to slip into the hands of Fiat management.

It was a moment which rivals had feared. Enzo Ferrari's irascible ways had played into their hands; it seemed inevitable that proper management control would marshal the team's potential and make Ferrari a devastating adversary. In fact it marked the beginning

◀ *Supporting a legend*

of a period of decline and upheaval, since Fiat executives, who knew nothing about the running of a racing team, lacked the passion and the immediacy of the gut decisions taken by the Old Man. Only recently has the Ferrari team begun to reorganize and regroup in a logical manner, but, such are the cumbersome procedures endemic to this motor racing institution, progress still tends to be infuriatingly slow.

And yet, despite the absence of success – they have not won a driver's championship since 1979 – Ferrari remains one of the most charismatic names in Grand Prix racing, a team driven by politics, glamour and the relentless expectancy of the Italian nation. During the past fifty years, Ferrari has become a graveyard, both literally and metaphorically, for some of the greatest names in Formula One. The competitive spirit engendered by the Old Man became too much for some and they pushed themselves beyond the limit. It was a curious contradiction. Ferrari loved his racing and yet he suffered untold grief when drivers died while pursuing glory in his name. For that reason, perhaps, Ferrari still arouses passion like no other team. For many, Ferrari *is* Grand Prix racing.

Born the younger son of a metal worker in the Po Valley in 1898, Enzo Ferrari had three ambitions: to sing opera at La Scala, to be a journalist and to race cars. A career on stage was a non-starter when it was discovered he did not have an ear for music. He did try sports writing but a limited vocabulary put journalism out of the question. So he settled for motor racing, but retired from the wheel at the age of thirty-four when his wife Laura gave birth to their only child, a son named Dino. Ferrari was not about to abandon his love affair with racing however, and he took to entering Alfa Romeos under the banner 'Scuderia Ferrari', a name which continues to stir the blood of motor racing enthusiasts sixty years later.

Ferrari still arouses passion like no other team

As for Ferrari himself, his blood reached boiling point in 1937. His role as official entrant for the Alfa Romeo team came to an end with a major disagreement over the manner in which the marque's future racing plans should be handled. Ferrari stormed out and decided to go his own way. Plans for the first Ferrari Grand Prix car had been laid by the end of 1939 but already the more menacing intentions of Herr Hitler were about to seriously affect life in Europe for the next five years.

Once hostilities had ceased motor racing began hesitantly, thanks to the shortage of cars, equipment and raw materials. It was a case of going racing with whatever came to hand. Ferrari made his first private foray in a major event at the 1948 Monaco Grand Prix with what, in essence, was a converted sports car manufactured by Ferrari's fledgeling company. The first proper Ferrari Grand Prix car, the Ferrari 125, appeared later in the year. Three were entered for the Italian Grand Prix but, not surprisingly, teething troubles hampered early progress with his purposeful-looking car.

Ferrari had won his first race when Giuseppe Farina headed the field in a minor race at Lake Garda in October 1948. Generally, though, Alfa Romeo had been sweeping the boards. When the Milanese company withdrew from racing in 1949, it left the way clear for Ferrari and Maserati. Ferrari immediately struck a mean blow when he signed Maserati's two leading drivers even though he already had two drivers of substance on his books. Apart from cutting the feet from beneath Maserati, it was the first sign of the Old Man's cunning when it came to manipulating his drivers in order to keep everyone on their toes.

The first major victory came when Alberto Ascari won the Swiss Grand Prix, one of nineteen races in which Ferraris, either in the hands of works drivers or privateers, had been entered that year. The calendar adopted a more meaningful format in 1950 when the sport's governing body introduced the World Championship, a competition which, apart from small adjustments over the years, has remained unchanged.

Alfa Romeo returned to dominate the 1950 season, but towards the end they received a jolt. Ferrari, having missed the occasional race while manufacturing and fine-tuning a brand new engine, were back on song and ready to challenge for the championship the following year.

In fact the first few races were nip and tuck, with the two Italian marques slogging it out, and Alfa Romeo just about retaining the upper hand. The British Grand Prix in July 1951 provided the dramatic turning point.

Alfa had entered four cars, Ferrari three. One of the cars from Maranello was driven by Froilan Gonzalez, the burly Argentinian having been given his chance by Enzo Ferrari. He seized it, quite literally, with both hands. It was an awe-inspiring sight as Gonzalez, chasing the Alfa Romeo of Juan Manuel Fangio, indulged in power slides at every corner. He seemed to be attempting to tear the steering wheel from its roots as he sat hunched in the cockpit, physically pushing the car faster than it cared to go. Ferrari had the upper hand in that the V12 was more frugal than Alfa's eight-cylinder. When Gonzalez won, finally ending Alfa's run of success, the big man was lifted bodily from the cockpit – quite a feat in itself – and the Ferrari team went wild. It was a historic moment, one which was represented for many years by a massive photograph in the hallway of the Ferrari headquarters.

That was the start of it. Ferraris finished first, third, fourth and fifth in Germany, followed by first and second in Italy. It was to be a double-edged sword. Alfa Romeo announced their withdrawal and, in doing so, more or less destroyed the chance of competitive racing in 1952. There was no one capable of providing Ferrari with decent competition. Fearing a red-wash, race organizers switched from Formula One to Formula

Two and the governing body nailed the lid on Formula One by granting these Formula Two events world-championship status.

Fortunately for Ferrari, he also had a very competitive Formula Two car; Alberto Ascari won six out of the seven rounds to give Ferrari his first championship. It was almost the same story in 1953, Ascari winning a 'mere' five of the eight Grands Prix that year to take the title for a second time. But along the way, motor racing enjoyed a classic battle on a high-speed triangle of public roads outside the French town of Reims.

Ferrari had signed Mike Hawthorn, a dashing young Englishman who smoked a pipe and enjoyed a pint of beer. Looking for all the world like a leftover from a wartime Spitfire base, Hawthorn was to make his name at Reims. He took on, and defeated, no less a person than Fangio. They ran neck-and-neck for lap after lap, a powerful duel with the twenty-four-year-old Surrey man forcing the 1951 World Champion to use every trick he

▲ *'Not quite in the condition she left the garage.' Eddie Irvine surveys the wreckage of his car after crashing during practice in Brazil*

54   **FERRARI**

knew to stay on terms. Hawthorn out-foxed the Argentinian at the last corner; it was the first Grand Prix victory for an Englishman since 1938.

Enzo Ferrari thought he was prepared for a change in engine formula for 1954 but his cars turned out to be difficult to drive, Ferraris picking up just two wins in championship Grands Prix. The difficulties continued into 1955, although Ferrari did collect a lucky win at Monaco when the opposition fell by the wayside. But all told, this was to be an unhappy season, Enzo being stunned when Ascari was killed while testing a Ferrari sports car.

It was a blow for the Lancia team, since Ascari had been their Formula One driver as they tried to make inroads into Grand Prix racing with a promising car. The loss proved too much for the struggling company, and halfway through 1955 the project was taken over by Ferrari, with help from the Italian Automobile Club and a considerable financial contribution from Fiat. It was a godsend for Ferrari since he had been hard-pressed to make his own cars competitive. Naturally, he played down that aspect and emphasized that he was doing this for the good of Italy.

Ferrari now had

a car capable

of tackling

Mercedes-Benz

The fact was, however, that Ferrari now had a car capable of tackling Mercedes-Benz, the German team which had dominated the scene more or less since their arrival the previous year. Things looked even better when Mercedes-Benz announced their withdrawal at the end of 1955, a move which left their star driver, Fangio, free to join Ferrari. The team went from strength to strength, Fangio winning his fourth world title, aided in part by Peter Collins (winner in Belgium and France), the Englishman handing over his car to Fangio in Italy in order to allow the maestro to gather enough points to put the championship beyond reach.

Then came another slump. Fangio left to join Maserati and won the championship for a fifth and final time. He drove a Maserati 250F, an exquisite car against which Ferrari had no answer; the team from Maranello failed to win a single championship Grand Prix in 1957.

The previous year, Enzo Ferrari had been strongly affected by the loss of his beloved son, Dino, whose death from muscular dystrophy and kidney failure turned him into a semi-recluse. He never recovered from the tragedy. A range of his road cars carried the name Dino, as would the neat little Grand Prix car entered for the 1958 season. Hawthorn used the Ferrari Dino 246 to win the championship, although it was a close call since he scored just one victory.

There was further tragedy when two top Italian drivers, Eugenio Castellotti and Luigi Musso, died in separate accidents at the wheel of Ferrari cars. Then two weeks after winning for Ferrari at Silverstone, Collins lost his life during the German Grand Prix.

Collins and Hawthorn had been great mates. As soon as he had clinched the title, Hawthorn retired from motor racing. Three months later, he was killed in a road crash near Guildford. There seemed no end to this catalogue of sorrow.

A new team of drivers was assembled for 1959: it was generally a disappointing year, although Tony Brooks came close to winning the championship. But if 1959 was poor, then 1960 was much worse, the front-engined Dino 246 being completely outclassed by the new generation of rear-engined, lightweight British cars from Cooper, Lotus and BRM.

Ferrari, meanwhile, had something just as striking taking shape for 1961, the year in which another change to the engine formula had been planned. This involved a reduction in engine size; the British manufacturers bitched and moaned about the low-power formula and Ferrari agreed with them outwardly while behind closed doors his engineers worked furiously on a new car and engine to suit the revised regulations.

The most distinctive aspect of the Ferrari was a twin-nostril nose, from which the car won the nickname Sharknose. This aerodynamic design was introduced in the interests of low drag, but the car's selling point lay behind the driver; the latest six-cylinder Dino engine had no equal in 1961. The Sharknose is generally considered to be one of the most attractive cars ever built by Ferrari, and yet not a single one survives. Ferrari adopted his familiar policy of paying no heed to history and scrapped his cars once they had outlived their usefulness. The record of the Sharknose in 1961 enhances its image, Ferrari winning the majority of races to take the title. But once again disaster intervened.

◄ **Michael Schumacher
and Niki Lauda:
Ferrari drivers from
different eras**

The championship had reached a terrible conclusion during the early stages of the Italian Grand Prix. The Ferrari of Wolfgang von Trips collided with another car on the back straight at Monza. The Ferrari speared off the track, careered up a bank and then cannoned off a spectator fence. Von Trips was killed, along with fourteen spectators. Phil Hill, driving a Ferrari, won the race and with it the championship but the success meant little to the sensitive American in the face of such tragedy.

The pendulum continued to swing the wrong way in 1962 when key engineers and managers walked out after disagreements with the obstinate Mr Ferrari. Then, to make matters worse, the British teams had sorted themselves out and found engines which were more than a measure for the Ferrari V6. The red cars did not win a single race that season; indeed, Enzo Ferrari withdrew his cars for the rest of the year following a dismal showing in his home Grand Prix.

Once again, however, Ferrari regrouped. Under the technical direction of Mauro Forghieri, a brilliant young engineer, a revised car was produced and John Surtees was hired to drive it. The former motorcycle world champion gave Ferrari their first championship Grand Prix victory for almost two years when he won in Germany in August 1963. Surtees continued to settle into the team and he was ready to make good use of another new car and engine the following year to collect the title, becoming the first and, to date, only man to win championships on two wheels and four. Then came another fallow year but, once again, Ferrari had his eye on the next change of engine formula, due to be introduced at the beginning of 1966.

With the British teams caught on the hop once more, Ferrari and Surtees were the clear favourites to win the championship. Then two races into the season Surtees walked out. Increasing discontent with the management had been exacerbated when he was refused the use of a nimbler hybrid car which would have been perfectly suited to the narrow streets of Monaco. Instead he had to make do with the latest car while the hybrid (one of the previous year's cars with a smaller engine) was entrusted to an Italian driver, Lorenzo Bandini.

Surtees won the next Grand Prix in Belgium, but that was his last for Ferrari before a major disagreement over driver pairings for the Le Mans twenty-four-hour race. A Ferrari driven by Ludovico Scarfiotti won the Italian Grand Prix in September, but by then a championship which was there for the taking had been thrown away thanks to internal strife.

Once again, it was a season of 'what might have been'

A commitment to sports car racing tended to marginalize the Formula One effort, particularly during the first half of the 1967 season. A three-car entry was sadly whittled down to just one when Bandini succumbed to terrible burns, received when he crashed at Monaco. Not long after, Scarfiotti withdrew from Formula One after seeing Michael Parkes' Ferrari crash heavily in Belgium and effectively end the Englishman's career. The young New Zealander Chris Amon, previously the junior in the team, was left to carry on single-handed in the majority of the remaining races, a heavy responsibility which he shouldered with remarkable equanimity.

Amon was joined in 1968 by the Belgian driver Jacky Ickx. Once again, it was a season of 'what might have been'. With sports car racing no longer on the agenda at Maranello, Ferrari concentrated on Formula One. Ickx won the French Grand Prix and a number of high placings put in him a position to become champion – until the throttle stuck open during the Canadian Grand Prix and caused him to crash and break his leg.

Amon's luck was appalling. He won four pole positions, led several races – and failed to win any. He ended 1969, the year Fiat bought 50 per cent of the company, leaving Enzo Ferrari in control of the racing, still searching for that elusive first victory. In Spain, for instance, he was holding a thirty-second lead when the engine failed.

Niki Lauda: acting as adviser to his old team ▶

◀ *The Ferrari refuelling team prepare for a pit stop*

Having had enough, he left the team in 1970 – just as Ferrari were about to turn over a new leaf.

A brand-new car and engine set Ferrari back on the winning trail with four victories at the end of the year – but too late to give Ickx a decent chance of winning the championship. And, in typical fashion, Ferrari would continue their winning form into 1971 – and then fade with reliability problems before the season was finished, thus squandering yet another opportunity to win the title. This was to mark the beginning of another major decline, designers coming and going as Enzo Ferrari, now under pressure from the Fiat board, sought to score points, never mind win races. Things went from bad to worse through 1972 and 1973, so much so that a complete reorganization was necessary for the following year.

Now began a superb period for the red cars bearing the black 'Prancing Horse' emblem. Under the young and energetic direction of Luca di Montezemolo, with the quizzically bespectacled Mauro Forghieri back in control of the technical department, Ferrari produced totally new cars and engines, to be driven by the hard-charging Clay Regazzoni and new boy Niki Lauda. Between them they won three times, and but for his inexperience Lauda might have become champion.

The young Austrian set the record straight with five wins in 1975, the result of diligent work on Ferrari's private test track, a unique facility which had been opened in

1971 on land adjoining the Ferrari factory. By relentless experimentation Lauda worked the Ferrari into a consistent winner and he seemed on course for a double championship in 1976 until a terrible accident at the Nürburgring in Germany.

He lost control and crashed, his car catching fire before being rammed by two others. He was given the last rites but, remarkably, was behind the wheel again six weeks later despite his head being swathed in bandages. In an epic struggle with James Hunt, he lost the title by a single point, but he was back in 1977 to prove what might have been. For three remarkable years, Ferrari set the standard and became the first Formula One team to put together a hat trick of consecutive Constructors' Championships.

Surprisingly – by Ferrari's erratic standards – the run continued, although not in quite the same dominant vein. 1978 brought five wins and second place in the Constructors' Championship, a hint that a downward spiral might be imminent. Not a bit of it. In 1979, Ferrari won both titles, Jody Scheckter holding the dubious honour of being the last driver to date to have become World Champion in a Ferrari.

The slump began in earnest in 1980 when Ferrari failed to cope successfully with 'ground effect', an aerodynamic phenomenon pioneered by the Lotus team and then copied by Williams and Brabham. Best results for Ferrari that season were three fifth places, Scheckter suffering the ignominy of failing to qualify for his penultimate race before retiring. The South African's departure left the way clear for his young team-mate, the brilliantly exuberant Gilles Villeneuve.

Driving for Ferrari is more than just a job ▶

It was at this time that Ferrari realized that the future lay in turbocharged engines, the first Ferrari turbo car being an ungainly device with brutal power. Villeneuve was one of the few drivers capable of controlling it. He actually managed to win two Grands Prix in 1981, one (Monaco) with a bit of luck and the other (Spain) by dint of his extraordinary reflexes and tenacity on a tight circuit where rivals, with nimbler but less powerful cars, could not find a way past the irrepressible French-Canadian.

Villeneuve's cheerful approach to life endeared him to the Old Man, a rare occurrence since Mr Ferrari increasingly liked to distance himself from his drivers, whom he considered to be no more than highly paid employees. Villeneuve was a force to be reckoned with, but for as long as Ferrari struggled to build a decent chassis to handle the prodigious turbo power rivals knew he would not be a consistent threat.

All that changed when Mr Ferrari, bowing to the inevitable, turned to British know-how and hired Dr Harvey Postlethwaite to design a state-of-the-art carbon-fibre chassis. Never mind that the Italians could not pronounce Harvey's surname; they spoke the same language when it came to returning Ferrari to the front in 1982. The new car looked every inch a winner; the championship beckoned. But life at Ferrari is never as simple as that. 1982 would be another year drenched in acrimony and sadness.

It took a while to hone the car into shape, but at the fourth round at Imola a political dispute robbed the field of most of the British entries, leaving the Ferraris to run the race as they pleased – or as one man pleased. Villeneuve had been joined the previous year by Didier Pironi, a talented Frenchman with an ice-cold temperament. Pironi won the race at Imola but, in doing so, went against team orders. Villeneuve, an honourable man not given to outward displays of emotion, was incensed. He vowed never to speak to Pironi again. Sadly, his threat would be fulfilled in the worst possible way.

During practice for the next race in Belgium, Pironi was the quicker of the two. Villeneuve went out for his last attempt, and during the course of the lap collided with a slow-moving car. The Ferrari cartwheeled at high speed, killing Villeneuve instantly when it nosedived into soft sand, the violent force breaking his neck. It was an appalling tragedy, one which affected Enzo Ferrari more than he cared to admit.

In Canada, Pironi looked set to dominate the race from pole position. He stalled at the start. A novice, coming through from the back of the grid, failed to see the stationary Ferrari and slammed into the back of it. Pironi leaped from the cockpit and attempted to rescue the hapless driver from a car which was now ablaze. It was to no avail since the initial impact had already caused fatal chest injuries.

Pironi lifted the team's morale by scoring consistent results good enough to put Ferrari back on course for the championship. Then, during practice for the German Grand

Prix at the end of July, Pironi crashed heavily after failing to see another car in pouring rain. The serious ankle injuries would end his motor racing career.

Not a man to allow sentiment to intrude too heavily, Mr Ferrari pressed on with plans to improve his team. A new headquarters and factory for the racing division had been built across the road from the production car plant to give Ferrari the most advanced motor racing facility of the day. It seemed inconceivable that they could fail to win. And yet . . .

Despite the misery of 1982, Ferrari had won the Constructors' Championship and they made it six in nine seasons when Patrick Tambay and René Arnoux scored four victories between them in 1983. But yet again, the driver's title slipped through their fingers due to an inability to cope quickly enough with the political and technical changes affecting the sport.

Things got worse the following year with just a single victory, continual modifications to the cars throughout the season indicating the growing state of turmoil. If the absence of success was becoming familiar, the team could not cope with the realization that the Ferrari engine, for so long their strongest card, was no longer powerful enough. Surges of competitiveness throughout 1984 and 1985 could not be sustained. Blame was shifted from department to department, none of which was helped by Enzo Ferrari becoming increasingly distant through illness.

◄ *Ferrari has the resources and the technology but internal politics continually put a brake on progress*

There were no wins at all in 1986 and just two at the end of the following season, by which time Mr Ferrari's health was causing more speculation than the prospects for his team. When the Old Man finally passed away in August 1988 his last decision, typically, brought success and angst in equal amounts. Grasping the nettle and offending traditionalists, Ferrari had hired the services of John Barnard, an Englishman whose considerable design skills had helped to lift McLaren from the doldrums to become a major force. The choice might have been acceptable had it not been for Barnard's insistence on operating from a new design office in Surrey rather than working at Maranello. Worse still, the actual chassis would be made in England under Barnard's direction. Such heresy!

Barnard answered his critics by producing a car which set new standards with a semi-automatic gearbox. Nigel Mansell christened it with a maiden victory in the 1989 Brazilian Grand Prix. Just as consistent success was within reach, political pressure drove Barnard out at the end of 1989 – almost at the very moment Alain Prost joined the driving team.

◀ *Tyres and pit signals
at the ready*

Barnard and Prost; it was the one combination which could have wiped the floor and yet the company had contrived to get rid of Barnard. As it was, Prost won five races in 1990 and came close to taking the championship. But just as matters appeared to be on the turn, the now ferocious Machiavellian atmosphere within the team proved too much for the Frenchman. After the penultimate race of the 1991 season, he compared the Ferrari with a truck – and was promptly sacked, leaving the team motoring nowhere with drivers who fell far below the required standard.

Ever since Ferrari's death, speculation had been rife over the identity of his successor. Montezemolo, the manager who had turned the team around with Lauda in the mid-1970s, had been moved on within the Fiat hierarchy before taking time out to master-mind Italia '90. But, now that he was free of football, the former lawyer was brought back to motor racing with orders to rescue Ferrari.

Montezemolo persuaded Barnard to return, brought Lauda on board as an adviser and hired Jean Todt (a Frenchman, no less) to manage the team. Then, for 1996, came the final act; paying a $25 million annual fee to secure the brilliance of Michael Schumacher. Once again, Ferrari was on course and about to climb from one of their many troughs.

The highs and lows have been dramatically different. Yet despite this Ferrari has been a consistent force since the start of the World Championship in 1950. It is this refusal to be crushed which has endeared the team just as much as the magic of one man's name.

'Enzo Ferrari was a *great* player,' recalls Harvey Postlethwaite. 'He was a great actor and like many men in that situation, he could orchestrate things exactly the way he wanted them. He was a hard user of people but he was totally passionate – and that is the right word – about the sport. It meant absolutely everything to him and that legacy will continue in Italy for as long as Ferrari goes motor racing.'

Paying a $25 million annual fee secured the brilliance of Michael Schumacher

FORTI

FORTI

FORTI

DRIVERS:

LUCA BADOER (ITALY)

ANDREA MONTERMINI (ITALY)

TEAM PRINCIPAL • GUIDO FORTI

CHIEF DESIGNER • PAOLO GUERCI

CAR • FORTI FG03

ENGINE • FORD V8

FIRST GRAND PRIX • BRAZIL, 1995

GRANDS PRIX CONTESTED • 17

WINS • 0

Forti became the 'in joke' of 1995. It was deemed to be clever to comment on how many times the bright yellow cars had been lapped during the course of a Grand Prix – assuming they were still running. It became fashionable among sports writers to make the Italian team a cause célèbre in the manner of Eddie the Eagle or Accrington Stanley. Forti Corse was the butt of superior paddock humour.

None of this was a surprise to the team. The owner, Guido Forti, had been in motor racing long enough to appreciate the competitive mentality which brooks no excuses. Forti had been highly successful in the lower formulas and now he was about to experience the opposite end of the spectrum in every sense.

Moving onto the peak of international motor racing with relatively little money and no background in Formula One could only mean one thing; a desperate struggle. Forti knew all that. But he still ventured into the cut-throat arena and, against all predictions, survived the 1995 season. He returned in 1996, not much better off financially, but still smiling. His argument was that Williams and McLaren had to start somewhere, so why not Forti Corse? If optimism could be bottled and sold, Forti would make a fortune.

In actual fact, what little money the fifty-three-year-old possessed at the beginning of 1995 had come from wheeling and successful dealing within the sport. Forti's name first reached the fringes of the limelight in 1975, when he backed Renzo Zorzi and the unknown Italian upset the form book by winning the prestigious Formula Three race at Monaco. Zorzi went on to briefly become a Formula One driver but Forti stayed put and won the Italian Formula Three championship four times between 1985 and 1989, his efficient team giving a leg-up to several hopefuls who became Grand Prix drivers.

Forti harboured the thought of Formula One himself, but first he needed to advance to Formula 3000, the final rung on the ladder before Grand Prix racing. Once again, his team was professional and successful, Forti Corse drivers winning nine times. Along the way, Forti took on board a young Brazilian driver who, while not exactly race-winning material, had enough backing to prompt the thought of going beyond Formula 3000.

Pedro Diniz comes from São Paulo, where his father made himself extremely wealthy by establishing a supermarket chain which would eventually cover Brazil and spread to Portugal and Spain. Such a power-base gave Diniz Senior impressive contacts within Brazilian business and he used those to tease out support for his son's motor racing exploits in Europe.

Like nearly all Brazilians, Diniz started in karting and progressed to Formula Ford and Formula Three. In 1991, at twenty-one, he arrived in England and spent two seasons

◀◀ Page 70:
Guido Forti (left):
'You've got to start
somewhere'

Forti had been

highly successful in

the lower formulas

FORTI

72

▲ *Life at Forti:*
a struggle for the team
and the drivers

racing in the British Formula Three series. A review of his first year in the weekly magazine *Autosport* said he had had 'a lot to learn . . . and the trouble is, he didn't make much progress.' A year later, the same magazine said he 'has clearly learned his lessons . . . the amiable Brazilian scoring a pair of fine third places.' Talk about damning with faint praise. To be considered of any use in Formula Three, you had to win – consistently. Diniz was far from championship material.

Nevertheless, a fat chequebook can easily cover a thin CV. Guido Forti signed him up for a season of Formula 3000 in 1993. Diniz managed a second place in France, but precious little else, one reviewer being moved to say that he was out of his depth. 1994 was not much better, but plans were already under way for a major project built around the Diniz family's wallet. The news that Forti Corse was about to enter Grand Prix racing was scarcely guaranteed to give Frank Williams sleepless nights.

◄ *Andrea Montermini's*
career marked time
in 1996

It was a desperately tall order. No more would Forti be able to buy a car from a manufacturer. In order to gain access to Formula One, he would have to design and build his own. To help him with the massive amount of organization involved, Forti had been joined by Carlo Gancia, a prominent figure in Brazilian motor racing who was also managing Diniz. Gancia became a co-owner of the team and looked after commercial affairs, a sensible arrangement since most of the money was coming from Brazil.

Forti shrugged off suggestions that he was taking an enormous risk. He said it would never be easy to enter Formula One but he was doing so now while some of the smaller Grand Prix teams were weak and he at least had the comfort of a reasonable budget – reasonable by Forti's standards but petty cash for the likes of Ferrari and McLaren.

A large portion of the funds went to the specialist business building the carbon-fibre chassis, and engines from Ford accounted for another sizeable chunk. Forti's existing factory at Alessandria, south of Milan, was more than adequate for the team to build up two cars, for Diniz and the experienced Roberto Moreno, and engineers and draughtsmen had been brought in to work on future developments, such as a semi-automatic gearbox, then de rigueur in Formula One, although for the time being the Forti-Fords relied on a manual gearbox, which in Grand Prix terms was like fitting a Ford Mondeo with an outside handbrake.

Contrary to predictions, the yellow cars were ready for the first race in Brazil. And, even more surprising, Diniz finished the race. He may have been tenth; he may have been last; he may have been lapped seven times by the winner; but such a result in his home Grand Prix brought emotional scenes. It was as if he had won the championship.

Forti was pleased. His cars may have been overweight and uncompetitive – but at least they were reliable. Damon Hill, for instance, had lost the lead when his rear suspension broke. There was hope for the future.

Both Fortis finished the third round of the championship in Italy, although as the season progressed they rarely got off the back row of the grid. Forti and Gancia had quickly realized that this was as good as the car was going to get. The Forti had been drawn by Sergio Rinland, a designer with considerable experience of Formula One. The only problem was, none of it was recent. The two parties soon fell out and the team was left to salvage what they could from an inherently uncompetitive chassis.

Over and out.
Luca Badoer makes
an unorthodox exit
from the cockpit
in Argentina ▼

Modifications were made here and there and the overall package was not helped by the Ford engine being . . . slow. This was the basic engine on the Ford shopping list; if Forti wanted more power, they would have to pay for it, and the budget was fully accounted for. There was also an increasing need to have the semi-automatic gearbox finished, but a lack of manpower and time meant tests could not be carried out. Practice for the Grands Prix effectively became test sessions, and each time the gearbox was tried the problems were such that it was not worth the risk of running the unit in the race.

Back-of-the-grid performances continued, the Fortis making the television screens each time they were lapped by the leaders. Which was often. 'Bloody hell!' exclaimed Damon Hill after a particularly busy Grand Prix. 'How many Fortis were out there today? Every five minutes, there was a yellow car. It seemed like there was about eight of them.'

Two-thirds of the way through the season rumours of Forti's demise gathered strength. It is a familiar routine which is applied to any team which appears to be wasting its time on a meagre budget. It certainly seemed likely that Forti would not make the expensive trip to the last two races in Japan and Australia. But come the hour, there they were, Diniz proving the point by rounding off the season with a distant seventh in Adelaide, the team's best placing.

Having got that far, however, the future did indeed seem bleak, on two counts. Diniz had been enticed away by the Ligier team for 1996, which was a blow to Gancia in particular since he had focused his efforts on the Brazilian. But worse than that, a new rule, due to come into force in 1996, was certain to crucify the little Italian team.

In a bid to clear the grid of cars which had no right to be there, a so-called 'One Hundred and Seven Per Cent Rule' would demand that any driver whose best lap time during qualifying was not within 107 per cent of the time established by the pole position man would not be permitted to start. In order words, Forti might go all the way to Australia and fail to make the first race of the season. Guido Forti gritted his teeth. No one said Grand Prix racing was easy. Rules is rules. Sure enough, neither driver qualified.

Diniz and Moreno had been replaced by Luca Badoer and Andrea Montermini, two drivers with Formula One experience. But even they could not haul the now grossly uncompetitive car towards anything resembling a decent lap time. Despite all that, however, the little team was far from disheartened. They had a $12 million budget and a staff of forty. Ferrari had three hundred people and an estimated $100 million. For Forti, however, such comparisons were irrelevant and fruitless. His next goal was the completion of a brand-new car in time for the first race in Europe. In the meantime, they would travel to São Paulo and Buenos Aires where, miraculously, both cars qualified,

Badoer finishing eleventh in Brazil and Montermini tenth in Argentina. They could hardly wait for the new car.

When it came, the 1996 Forti was scarcely the answer. There was only one at first for Badoer, then Montermini wrote his off during an exploratory practice session in the wet on race morning in Monaco. It was an ill-advised move because Monaco had been the only occasion when Montermini had qualified in the three European races thus far. Now he would not be able to start on a day when only three cars would reach the chequered flag. A septuagenarian in a golf buggy could have scored points. A team's first season is carried along by novelty and hope; any shortcomings are easily excused. Here was proof that it is usually the second year when the reality begins to bite.

Formula One is nothing if not surprising. Just when it seemed that Forti was struggling on the road to nowhere, they turned up at the next race in Spain dressed to

Back row brigade in 1996 ▼

Another embarrassing

exit ▶

kill. The cars were no longer yellow but smartly turned out in green and white. The team personnel were sporting crisp new uniforms. Forti had become a part of Shannon Racing.

Just who was Shannon Racing? It was like asking for the home address of the head of the FBI. New backing had come from the Finfirst finance group, which as far as anyone knew was Irish registered and Italian based with funds coming from somewhere else. Finfirst was also said to own Sokol, a company manufacturing helicopters in eastern Europe.

As for their associate company, Shannon Racing, they were running no less than thirteen Formula Three cars in Europe and two cars in the Formula 3000 International Championship. That was a substantial undertaking in anyone's book. Nothing shines like new money. The Fortis were gleaming in Spain and a new series of jokes was about to start.

JORDAN

JORDAN

DRIVERS:

RUBENS BARRICHELLO (BRAZIL)

MARTIN BRUNDLE (ENGLAND)

TEAM PRINCIPAL • EDDIE JORDAN

CHIEF DESIGNER • GARY ANDERSON

CAR • JORDAN 196

ENGINE • PEUGEOT V10

FIRST GRAND PRIX • UNITED STATES, 1991

GRANDS PRIX CONTESTED • 81

WINS • 0

Just before Christmas 1994, Eddie Jordan attended a book signing session in Dublin. The publication told the story of his Formula One team and the bookstore expected a reasonable turnout. This, after all, was the tale of a local boy who had made good in the glamorous world of Grand Prix racing; an Irishman with a success story to tell. The fact that his team had yet to win a Grand Prix was irrelevant. As with all things in Ireland, it was sufficient that he could talk a good race; Eddie Jordan was World Champion ten times over at that particular game.

The bookshop felt they had covered all eventualities by ordering 400 copies, which they stacked high in the window. The session was supposed to last for an hour, during which time they might, if they were lucky, work through a fair number of books. Mr Jordan would arrive at 10.30 a.m. sharp. He would then be free to leave by 11.30 a.m., latest. They said he was pressed for time. They were wrong on every count.

Eddie Jordan was twenty minutes late. Mild panic had begun to set in because the queue stretched out of the shop and snaked its way to the entrance of the shopping mall. There was relief all round when the slightly built figure bustled into the shop, offered sincere apologies and smoothed ruffled feathers within minutes. There followed a non-stop dialogue with the customers as they filed through, offering their best wishes for the 1995 season and asking pertinent and well-informed questions. Many were dressed in Jordan team gear and were delighted by the banter when Jordan asked loudly: 'And how much did we rip you off for that?' He was beaming broadly. He wasn't joking.

The queue was never-ending. Old friends, pals from the Irish racing scene, former girlfriends; Jordan knew them all. He might not have been able to remember their names immediately but that shortfall was lost in the fast flow of chat.

'Are you still racing that ropy old Formula Ford?' he asked one man. 'You know, the one I sold you . . . ' A middle-aged purchaser, clutching a copy of the book, shuffled forward. 'Hello, Declan, how are you?' said Jordan, stretching out his hand. 'Hello, EJ . . . It's Dominic,' grinned the man. 'Indeed you are,' quipped Jordan, with barely a pause for breath.

'Jayzus, I remember you all right,' he said to an attractive woman in her late thirties. 'In the back of a Cortina down Dollymount Strand.' Gales of laughter all round. The morning swept past in a swirl of Irish warmth and repartee. Every book was sold, fans rushing to rival shops in search of copies. Jordan eventually left the shop at 12.45 a.m. The bookstore said they had never seen the like.

That cameo said everything about the standing of a Grand Prix team built on the gregarious personality of one man. The only unusual aspect of the occasion was that

◄◄ Page 82:
Jordan: a team built around the gregarious personality of one man

This was the tale of a local boy who had made good

▲ *A typically spectacular*
Jordan smokescreen

Jordan had not received remuneration for his time and neither would he earn a penny from copies sold. It would be a subject about which he would, in good humour, frequently remind the author, but more than anything Jordan's effort that morning illustrated his basic decency and an awareness of the value of good public relations. It was also indicative of a strong attachment to the Old Country.

There is a distinct sense of 'Irishness' about Jordan's team. Dublin brogue flows constantly from the boss's office, and the technical director, the accountant, the team manager and the sponsor liaison officer provide accents from different parts of the Emerald Isle. Formed in 1990, Jordan Grand Prix is one of the newest Formula One teams on the scene but such has been the impression made that it seems as though Jordan's operation has been around for much longer. Certainly, Jordan Grand Prix is rated as a top team. Eddie Jordan has come a long way in a remarkably short space of time.

There is some sort of irony in the fact that a strike by Irish bank officials led Jordan into a business worth millions. Until the Republic's fiscal system became close to breakdown in 1970 as bank clerks sought more pay, Jordan had no interest in fast motoring.

Cars were a means to an end as this mercurial twenty-two-year-old rushed from his home in Bray to wherever the next deal could be done.

His career as such had no positive direction. Dentistry had been tried and rejected. Now he was studying Cost and Management Accountancy at the Dublin College of Commerce while working for the Bank of Ireland. It was a reasonable enough job and the prospects were good. But lurking at the back of Jordan's intensely enquiring mind was the thought that the next opportunity could be the great one.

He didn't know what it would be about or where it might lead; just that it would be tremendous. There are no half measures with Eddie Jordan.

Such romantic idealism was a part of his cheerful optimism as he set off for the Channel Islands to seek temporary employment as the strike took hold. While in Jersey,

Jordan promised much at the start of the 1996 season but failed to deliver ▼

he came across a go-kart race at Bouley Bay. These noisy, knee-high devices with their tiny wheels may represent the lower echelons of a thrilling sport but they hurled Eddie Jordan into a world where, two decades later, he was vying for space at the very top. That go-kart race was the catalyst for Ireland's first Formula One team although Jordan, even at the height of his remarkable optimism, would never have believed he would own it. Drive for it, maybe. But where would he find the wherewithal to run it? In 1970 he hardly had two coins to rub together.

Financial constraints aside, nothing would do until Eddie had tried his hand. He clubbed together enough money to buy a kart on his return to Dublin and, in every sense of the expression, he quickly became Irish champion. That done, there was no question about making the next step into 'proper racing cars'. Jordan's competitive juices were at full flow.

There is no shortage of motor sport events on both sides of the border, but even so racing in Ireland has its limitations. Jordan won several events in Formula Ford, the junior category for single-seater racing cars, but the need for new challenges took him 'across the water' on several occasions to enter races in England. It was one such visit which almost brought an end to his career in late 1975 when a major accident at the Mallory Park circuit in Leicestershire sidelined him for most of the following season.

Eddie Jordan Racing was formed in 1980 in a lock-up garage

But the bug had truly bitten and a move into a more powerful single-seater series brought him the 1978 Irish Formula Atlantic Championship. In case anyone wanted to know, Eddie was making it clear that from here on in he was expecting to become the first Irish World Champion.

Eddie's girlfriend, Marie McCarthy, had become accustomed to such enthusiastically articulated claims. She had heard it all before. In fact, she was used to chat of various kinds thanks to playing basketball for Ireland and working as a settler for Floods the bookmakers before joining the chartered accountants Price Waterhouse. Marie gave all of that up when she and Eddie decided to marry in 1979 and set sail for England, where her husband was intent on a substantiating his claim to fame.

Eddie Jordan Racing was formed in 1980 in a lock-up garage at the Silverstone circuit. Marie worked as a £40 per week packer at a local factory before giving birth to the first of four children. It was a hand-to-mouth existence but enjoyable nonetheless as Marie and baby Zoe shared a caravan and the unique experiences which came with criss-crossing Europe as Eddie took part in as many Formula Three races as he could afford during a hectic summer.

Looking back now those were halcyon days, although at the time it was a case of not knowing where the next punt was coming from. Jordan smiled, persuaded and flattered,

talking his way into the right places. At Monaco one year, while taking part in the Formula Three race which supported the classic Formula One event, Eddie wangled tickets for the Grand Prix Ball. His mechanic doubled as babysitter in the caravan. Marie, wearing a frock bought from Oxfam, felt and looked a million dollars while her husband made the most of an opportunity to rub shoulders with the sport's senior power-brokers. Eddie got as far as testing a Formula One car for the McLaren team. Little did he realize, even in his wildest dreams, that thirteen years later a team under the Jordan name would be vying with McLaren for fourth place in the 1994 World Championship.

Realism of a different sort was taking hold as Eddie began to accept that perhaps he did not have the necessary skills as a top-line driver. But all was not lost because there was pleasure to be had from wheeling and dealing even if personal satisfaction sometimes outweighed the financial gain. Eddie's loquacious gifts stood him in good stead as a motivator and manager; it quickly became clear that he would be better off running a team and gambling his capital than driving a racing car and risking his limbs. At the end of 1981 he quietly retired as a racing driver.

The Jordan family had moved into a five-bedroomed house in Silverstone village, the ideal place for Marie to take in lodgers, most of whom were prospective young racing drivers chasing dreams in the manner of their new landlord. Meanwhile, Jordan's team had become established as a serious entrant in the Formula Three scene in Europe. Jordan, who prides himself on his talent-spotting ability, was one of the first team owners to give Ayrton Senna a trial in a Formula Three car. In the event, Senna went to another team and Jordan's driver, Martin Brundle, finished runner up to the great Brazilian after a brilliant struggle in the British championship in 1983.

When Formula 3000 – a series for scaled down Grand Prix cars – came into being in 1985, Jordan moved his team up another level and eventually won the championship with Jean Alesi, later to become a Ferrari driver. All the while, Eddie had his eye on Formula One and Grand Prix racing. It seemed like typical Jordan hyperbole. Suddenly Marie realized he was serious.

'He started to put together a plan to run a Grand Prix team in 1991,' says Marie. 'This involved total commitment. It was to be the toughest time for all of us because we stood to lose everything – our latest house [a stone-built cottage with a pool, tennis court and immaculate gardens], the lot – if this didn't work. I never really thought I was the nervous type but my hands came out in spots, you know, thinking about selling the house, where to school the kids, things like that. But this was what Eddie really wanted to do. It was driving him on. I knew there was no way it would be anything other than this.'

◄ *Jordan: noted for its 'Irishness'. Team manager John Walton (left) and technical director Gary Anderson*

Grand Prix insiders were sceptical. It was one thing for Jordan to buy his Formula Three and Formula 3000 cars from a manufacturer such as Reynard; quite another to actually design and build his own. Jordan was operating out of a small industrial unit attached to the Silverstone racetrack; he would need a place ten times that size if he was to be taken seriously. Jordan's persuasive talk had taken him this far. But now he had to put up or shut up. Typically, he did the former and paid no heed to the latter.

It cost £2.5 million to launch the team – Jordan Grand Prix – into the sixteen-race season. From the moment of Jordan's first public appearance, in Phoenix, Arizona, the hard-bitten world of Formula One was impressed. Jordan's pedigree as a successful entrant shone through. His team was professionally turned out and the green Jordan-Fords, with backing from 7-Up, looked neat and workmanlike. It was clear that Jordan Grand Prix was not a makeweight team in the manner of many newcomers to this fast-moving and expensive game.

The cars were the work of Gary Anderson, a burly Ulsterman who had made the most of an immensely practical approach fashioned by twenty years spent working as a Formula One mechanic. This was typical of Jordan's adventurous style, not to mention

The Jordan team's ability to attract different sponsors produced this mouthful on Barrichello's visor ▶

his kinship with anyone from back home. Anderson had worked his way up to the role of chief mechanic with the McLaren team before switching to Indycar racing in the USA, where he applied his engineering know-how rather than expertise with wrenches and spanners. But he had never designed anything as grand as a Formula One car. It was a gamble Jordan was prepared to take.

Full justification of that controversial choice came when Jordan-Fords finished in the top six on a number of occasions. Anderson had earned the respect of his peers. Indeed a Jordan would have finished second in the Belgian Grand Prix but for an engine problem. As it was, a tearful Eddie Jordan had celebrated his first championship points in Canada, the team gathering thirteen in total at the end of a dream first year.

The honeymoon period came to an embarrassing halt in 1992 when Jordan scored but one point after struggling home in sixth place in the final race of the season. The hiatus had been caused by one of Eddie Jordan's few tactical errors. Ford engines had cost the team £4.3 million in 1991. For 1992, Jordan had done a deal with Yamaha. Eddie liked the fact that the engines were free. But they were also gutless and unreliable. It almost brought Jordan Grand Prix to its knees.

Gambling once more, Jordan signed Rubens Barrichello, a virtually unknown twenty-year-old Brazilian, and switched to engines built by Brian Hart, a hugely talented independent based in Essex. It took most of 1993 for the new partnership to gel and, when it did so, the results were spectacular. Jordan finished fifth and sixth in the Japanese Grand Prix, an impressive performance in itself during a rain-interrupted race but one made more noteworthy by the efforts of the team's latest recruit.

This was the first Grand Prix for Eddie Irvine and yet he drove like a veteran in the treacherous conditions. Once again, Eddie Jordan had speculated by giving the man from County Down his chance when, on paper, he had little to show for a lurking natural talent. Irvine had responded magnificently by not only finishing sixth to score a point but also showing that he was not in the least over-awed by such lofty company, a precocious attitude which had brought him to blows with Ayrton Senna in a much-publicized post-race interview. Eddie Jordan's only regret seemed to be that he had missed the publicity after dashing off as soon as the Grand Prix had finished. But he stood by his man, so much so that Irvine was signed to partner Barrichello for 1994.

The team was now ready to move forward, thanks not only to a strong driver line-up but also to a management restructuring in which John Walton, who had worked as a mechanic for Jordan in his Formula Three days, was made team manager. The Dubliner possessed a perfect understanding of his job and, just as important, of his employer. Walton and Jordan spoke the same language in every sense, Walton's calm nature the perfect foil for Jordan's sometimes excitable excesses.

Barrichello scored Jordan's first pole position in Belgium

The team, with fifty-two employees still essentially a compact unit compared to almost four times that number at McLaren and Ferrari, went from strength to strength. Barrichello finished on the podium for the first time in Japan and scored Jordan's first pole position in Belgium. At the end of the season, the team with the 'Discover Ireland' logos prominently displayed on drivers and cars alike finished fifth in the Constructors' Championship, a brilliant achievement on a comparatively meagre Formula One budget of £11 million.

Jordan's efforts had not gone unnoticed. Peugeot, who had come into Formula One as an engine supplier for McLaren in 1994, decided to switch to the Irish team. This was an important nod of approval from a major motor manufacturer; it was another step in Jordan's master plan to do battle with the big names.

Jordan expanded his team in an attempt to raise his game to match the expectations. Now operating on a budget of £13.4 million (and no longer having to pay for his engines), Jordan attracted backing from Total, the international oil and gas company, Marlboro, the world's best-selling cigarette brand, Beta, a respected hand-tool company from Italy, and

another twenty-two companies ranging from a paint manufacturer to a market leader in writing instruments.

Much of this marketing success was down to the effectiveness of Jordan's commercial manager, Ian Phillips, another shrewd appointment by Jordan at the start of his Formula One campaign. Phillips had impeccable credentials, not in marketing as such but in the ways of the motor racing world. A former editor of *Autosport* magazine, the weekly bible of the sport, Phillips had gone on to serve his time in management with the Donington circuit and then a now-defunct Formula One team. His sense of news value had been unbeaten anywhere and, in his new role, he could sniff a potential sponsor almost before the company concerned had begun to think about it.

They made a formidable team, Jordan and Phillips, as they took prospective backers more or less by storm. Whereas the likes of McLaren went in for the smooth, textbook approach which could last for months, Jordan and Phillips would win on up-front

◄ *Martin Brundle had a dreadful start to 1996 but his experience soon shone through*

honesty and the excitement generated by 'the deal'. Negotiations were generally quick and good-natured. They made no bones about the status of the team. Jordan is on the way up, they would say, but don't expect us to win. Not yet, anyway.

It was a realistic assessment even though the pressure to improve was increasing dramatically. 1995 turned out to be difficult enough as a series of mechanical problems let the team down and proved just how stretched the technical department continued to be. Anderson was deeply frustrated because Eddie Jordan was attempting to talk big when, quite patently, the reality was very different. It was physically impossible given the structure of the team, which, despite Jordan's plans, had actually remained more or less unchanged.

There was a high point in Canada when Barrichello and Irvine finished an excellent second and third, the first time that two Jordan drivers had been on the podium, but generally it was a case of what might have been, the Jordan drivers failing to finish twenty

times. The team ended the year with twenty-one points, seven less than the previous year and twenty short of the target Jordan had set. Never mind. There was always next season.

Jordan's optimism is incurable. After the 1995 British Grand Prix – during which both drivers had once again qualified well but failed to make anything of it because of technical problems – Eddie Jordan literally swung into action. A professional friend of the famous, he made much of his acquaintance with various pop stars. Chris Rea, an out and out racing fan, frequently made the Jordan motorhome his base and Eddie would talk when the right moment arose – which, in his estimation, was quite often – about his friendship with members of U2.

Jordan retains an interest in pop music and that has been demonstrated each year at Silverstone by a rock party supplied courtesy of Jordan Grand Prix. At the close of

Jordan ought to have had the legs of the troubled Ferrari team in 1996. Barrichello leads Schumacher ▼

business a trailer is pulled into the paddock to act as a temporary stage for a fully-amplified band made up of members of the motor racing circus willing to have a go. It is, as Jordan would say, 'seriously good music'. Williams' Damon Hill is a regular, letting off steam through his love of guitar playing. The entire scene, fuelled by beer and Guinness laid on by Jordan, is typical of the team's *joie de vivre*; a throwback to the more relaxed days of Formula One. Of course Jordan derives great pleasure from the fact that his antics irritate the more serious-minded members of the Formula One paddock in much the same way that Ian Phillips, with his host of happy sponsors, knows that a Jordan covered with stickers is not the image which the Formula One élite would prefer.

As time goes by, however, the dilemma for Jordan has become more acute. This is a team founded on frankness and an absence of bullshit. The media has forgiven Jordan many things, simply because Eddie and his boys are 'good lads'. Jordan Grand Prix is one of the most popular of the top band of teams, an image which is assisted greatly by the professional, no-nonsense approach of Jordan's press officer, Louise Goodman.

In the background there is a continual push to improve and be talked about in the same breath as Williams, Ferrari and Benetton, but the next step is massive, one which threatens to tear Jordan from its roots. Jordan insists he will not change. The trouble is, he may have no choice.

At the beginning of 1996 a major sponsorship deal was announced with Benson and Hedges. Finally everything was in place. Jordan had a works engine deal with the rapidly improving Peugeot Sport team in Paris and now he had the money to fund the test and development plans which Gary Anderson had always wanted. The expectation was higher than ever and yet, in the first half of the season, Jordan had scored a mere handful of points. Now the cars were reliable but the team was being let down by accidents (not always the fault of the drivers) and minor problems which should have been ironed out.

Jordan remains philosophic, talking quietly out of the side of his mouth about how he's maybe going to 'sneak a win' one day. He knows that will be about the height of his aspirations unless the team changes and threatens to lose some of the identity he cherishes so much. But Jordan will not dwell on his problems. He will immediately switch to attack, demanding to hear the latest gossip. Invariably he knows it all. Indeed, on one famous occasion, he instigated a scurrilous tale just to see how long it would take to get back to the Jordan motorhome.

Then he is into the sports results. What about Oxford United (his adopted home town)? What about the golf? He devours the score card, paying particular attention to the Irish players. He knows them all. Of course.

LIGIER

LIGIER

DRIVERS:

OLIVIER PANIS (FRANCE)

PEDRO DINIZ (BRAZIL)

TEAM PRINCIPAL • GUY LIGIER

CHIEF DESIGNER • FRANK DERNIE

CAR • LIGIER JS43

ENGINE • MUGEN-HONDA V10

FIRST GRAND PRIX • BRAZIL, 1976

GRANDS PRIX CONTESTED • 310

WINS • 8

When Ligier won the 1996 Monaco Grand Prix, there was genuine pleasure along the pit lane. Not two months before, the French team had been written off. Closure seemed imminent. The victory, Ligier's first in fourteen years, was typical of the varying fortunes of a team which is quintessentially French, a survivor of times which have been lean more often than triumphant.

Even though Ligier have been around for a mere two decades, their absence would be regretted. In a paddock which is dominated by British and Italian influences Ligier are perceived as racing for the glory of La France even though the team's structure has been infiltrated by people who can barely speak the language, never mind drink brandy and smoke untipped Gitanes.

Such colourful habits are part of the founder's repertoire. Guy Ligier had been a keen sportsman, rowing in national championships before switching to rugby and playing hooker for Racing Club of Vichy, the town where he was born in 1930. Ligier represented the French military by playing for the 1st XV before taking up motorcycle racing and winning the French 500cc championship in 1959 and 1960.

A switch to car racing was so unsuccessful that he quit the sport for a couple of years before reappearing in 1963. Driving mainly sports cars, but with outings in Formula Two, Ligier enjoyed moderate success before deciding to turn his hand to Formula One in 1966.

It was possible at the time to buy a second-hand Grand Prix car and go motor racing – in a manner of speaking. The car Ligier acquired – a Cooper-Maserati – was not quick in the hands of the works drivers. With the burly Frenchman on board, the lumbering car went even slower. The following year, however, Ligier proved it was not necessarily the fault of the machinery when, using money made from his construction company, he purchased an ex-works Brabham – the car which had won the 1966 championship – and achieved little of note, apart from a championship point for finishing sixth in the German Grand Prix. His was very much the operation of a privateer, as highlighted by an incident during practice for the Mexican Grand Prix.

The Brabham had ground to a halt at the side of the track, Ligier believing that the engine had blown up. Leaving his junior mechanic to retrieve the car and get on with repairs, the boss went to the local hospital with his senior mechanic, who had been taken ill. The young mechanic was some way into the process of swapping engines when it was discovered that the car had actually run out of petrol. The air was blue when M. Ligier returned and discovered this latest turn in events. That would be Ligier's last Grand Prix and, after a couple of abortive outings in Formula Two, it seemed a better option for Ligier to turn his hand to industry and the manufacture of performance cars.

◄◄ Page 100:

Oliver Panis: surprise

winner in Monaco

The victory was

Ligier's first in

fourteen years

LIGIER

▲ *Panis presses on.*
Despite changes in
management structure,
French blue has
remained to the fore
on the Ligiers

Automobiles Ligier was founded in Vichy in 1969. The first competition sports car was known as the JS1, a tribute to his close friend Jo Schlesser, who had been killed during the previous year's French Grand Prix. Ligier and Schlesser had been business partners as well as sharing the winning Ford GT40 in the twelve-hour endurance race at Reims in 1967. Although Ligier directed the efforts of his new company towards sports car racing in general and Le Mans in particular, the pull of Formula One would prove too difficult to resist.

The idea of building a Grand Prix car became a reality when Ligier won sponsorship from SEITA, the French tobacco company which marketed Gitanes cigarettes. SEITA's previous involvement with Matra, the aerospace company which had built and raced

Grand Prix and sports cars in the past, helped Ligier gain access to the Matra twelve-cylinder engine and with it came Gerard Ducarouge, a colourful engineer who would assist with the design of the car and general running of the Ligier Formula One team.

The first Ligier Grand Prix car, the JS5, was unveiled in October 1975. It was a striking machine, not so much because of its light-blue paint scheme and Gitanes identification as because of a massive nostril-like airbox mounted on top of the engine. This, combined with a broad nose, led immediately to the use of Teapot as a nickname for the all-French car.

Jacques Laffite, jolly and slightly built, contributed to the curious image but the seriousness of the effort was soon evident when he finished fourth in the team's third race. Changes to the regulations forced the abandonment of the 'teapot' engine cover during the season but the revision did not affect performance unduly, Laffite taking second place with a new car in the Austrian Grand Prix and contributing to a worthy fifth place for Ligier in the 1976 Constructors' Championship.

The team's first win – through merit and good fortune jointly, when the leading Lotus ran low on fuel – came in Sweden the following year but the momentum began to fall away in 1978 when SEITA had worries over tobacco advertising and Matra decided to withdraw their raucous V12 engines at the end of the season. Ligier finished the year sixth in the Constructors' Championship. Times change quickly in Grand Prix racing. Just four months later and two races into the 1979 season, Ligier seemed poised to win everything in sight.

The decision had been made to run a two-car team for the first time. Laffite had been joined by fellow-countryman Patrick Depailler, an equally carefree character who contributed greatly to the haze of cigarette smoke created by M. Ligier in the team motorhome. When the season kicked off in South America, the Ligiers finished one-two in Argentina and Brazil. Laffite won on both occasions and no other team could get a look in.

In the absence of team orders, Depailler was keen to maintain his chances of winning the driver's title. He led Laffite in Spain and Jacques's strenuous efforts, while running in his team-mate's slipstream, resulted in a blown engine, Ligier having switched to the normally reliable Ford-Cosworth DFV at the beginning of the season.

When Depailler crashed heavily during the next race in Belgium, the team was incapable of rebuilding the car to the same competitive standard. Suddenly Ligier seemed to be losing its way, and matters were not helped when Depailler broke his legs after crashing into a cliff face while hang-gliding. SEITA, continuing to support the team through Gitanes, insisted on a French-speaking driver as a replacement. Jacky Ickx was

LIGIER

chosen despite not having completed a full season of Formula One racing for five years. And it showed. For all the good Ickx did, Ligier effectively became a one-car team – and even Jacques Laffite was struggling.

The fall from early season dominance was remarkable. Politics were further to blame when Guy Ligier chose to abandon the wind tunnel his designers had used regularly in favour of a government-run facility at St-Cyr. The baselines for important calculations were upset by the move. That was one excuse given for the sudden loss of form.

The other, more unofficial reason was that Gerard Ducarouge had but sketchy details of the car set-ups used in South America. Legend has it that he wrote his notes on the back of a Gitanes pack – and then lost the packet. That may be an apocryphal tale but it certainly fitted the rather haphazard method of going motor racing at Equipe Ligier Gitanes. At the end of a season which had promised so much, Laffite could only manage fourth place in the drivers' championship.

▲ Jacques Laffite (left), a Ligier stalwart, chats with Danielle Audetto who worked briefly for the team as a liaison officer

It was a similar story in 1980 as the team shot itself in the foot with remarkable regularity. Once again the championship effort was diluted as Laffite and his new partner, Didier Pironi, contrived to take points from each other. And when the drivers were not fighting among themselves, race victories which were there for the taking were frittered away by ineffective management decisions.

The French and the British Grands Prix, run mid-season, were classic examples. A Ligier was on pole position for both and led comfortably but each time a technical problem cost the French team dearly. And, in the midst of this drama, Ducarouge was running around like a demented soul. Race morning in France, for example, brought scenes of a harassed team which had been up all night after a fuel leak had been discovered on Laffite's car, Ducarouge adding to the tension by having a gantry carrying airlines come crashing down on his immaculately coiffured head. And, in the midst of this, a film crew making an advertisement for Gitanes! Small wonder that the orderly Williams team in the pit next door knew their moment would come if they did their homework correctly and then waited long enough. Sure enough, the chastened Ligiers finished second and third at home after the crafty Alan Jones had moved his Williams into the lead at two-thirds distance.

Laffite and his new partner, Didier Pironi, contrived to take points from each other

At the end of the season, Ligier were second in the Constructors' Championship. But Williams had scored almost twice as many points. Ligier could have won in Argentina, Brazil, Monaco, France, Britain and Canada. Instead, they only collected maximum points in Belgium and Germany. It was absolutely typical of Ligier's method of working.

The barely controlled turmoil continued into 1981. A return to the Matra V12 took the team back a step or two, added to which Jean-Pierre Jabouille was chosen to replace Pironi even though he had not fully recovered from an accident at the end of the previous season. A sudden politically motivated technical change to the cars affected Ligier more than their rivals, and yet the irony was that Laffite found himself with an outside chance of winning the championship, come the final round in Las Vegas. He failed, but at least the chirpy Frenchman had the satisfaction of two well-worked victories to his name that season, the final one – Canada in October 1981 – being the last time Ligier would reach the top of the podium for fourteen years.

When Ducarouge had left the team design was in the hands of less well-known engineers, who took some time to develop a controversial interpretation of the technical rules governing side-skirts on the 1982 cars. When the new Ligiers finally appeared at Monaco the scrutineers ordered important sections of the bodywork to be removed, thus taking away a major chunk of the promised performance advantage which the team had spent months trying to achieve. There was a fair amount of table-thumping in the Ligier motorhome that day as Le Patron laid into the best cognac and anyone who cared to question the wisdom of it all.

Laffite and his team-mate, Eddie Cheever, picked up enough points for Ligier to claim eighth place in the constructors' table. That would be seen as a result twelve months later, after the team, now without Laffite and struggling with a Ford DFV as the turbo era got into its stride, had failed to score any points at all. Guy Ligier, meanwhile, was pulling a few strokes in order to get his hands on a turbocharged engine.

In the early Sixties, Ligier's civil engineering company had been involved with public contracts, primarily in motorway construction. The good times were severely curtailed by a shift in government politics. An outraged Ligier, despite his right-wing tendencies, threw his weight behind an ambitious young left-wing deputy from the Vichy region. His name was François Mitterrand. They became good friends and Guy's support would pay handsome dividends.

Mitterrand had been one of the witnesses at the marriage of Ligier's daughter in 1982, and a year later the politician applied discreet pressure to the state-owned Régie Renault to supply their turbocharged engines to Ligier in 1984.

Gaining access to the V6 was one thing; making the most of it quite another. The team continued their shambling ways and it was not until the return of Laffite in 1985 that any sort of progress looked like being maintained. Indeed, there had been other changes within the company, most notably the arrival of Gerard Larrousse and Michel Tetu, former Renault employees who brought organizational and design skills respectively.

The results began to trickle through, although the placing of the erratic Italian Andrea de Cesaris in the second car was not seen as a good move, particularly when he completed a neat barrel-roll which won Guy Ligier prime-time television news coverage he could well have done without. He was dismissed, his place being taken by Philippe Streiff, who then came close to emulating him in the last race of the season in Australia. With the Ligiers running second and third in the final stages, Streiff took it upon himself to relieve his team-mate of second place. The two cars collided. Laffite maintained his position and Streiff just managed to crawl home with his front suspension severely deranged. The same condition might have applied to the irascible Guy Ligier had neither of his cars made it to the flag.

Despite yet another chequered season, hopes were high for 1986. But then came a crippling blow in every sense. Seconds after the start of the British Grand Prix at Brands Hatch, there was chaos when an Arrows spun across the pack, cars going in all directions. A Ferrari veered to the right and Laffite, venturing alongside, had no option but to do

◀ *Pedro Diniz: the man with the money*

likewise and head down a gentle grassy slope. But whereas the Ferrari managed to duck round the edge of a stout barrier protecting the mouth of a tunnel running under the track, Laffite crashed straight into the metal rails. The front of the Ligier folded and Guy Ligier's most faithful servant suffered severe leg injuries which would end his Formula One career.

The second half of the season went by without further incident – indeed, without anything of note. And just when things looked as though they couldn't get worse, they invariably did. The results in 1987 were catastrophic, the season getting off badly when a deal to run an Alfa Romeo turbo was jeopardized by a Ligier driver, René Arnoux, making disparaging remarks about the engine. It gave Alfa Romeo a handy get-out, and even though Ligier sued, the boys in blue were left with a late start and a customer BMW engine to power them further down the road of mediocrity.

A switch to the straightforward Judd engine the following year brought, for some reason, a strange car which one technical reviewer described as 'heavy and over-complicated'. Having scored just a single point in 1987, Ligier went one better in 1988 and scored none at all. There was a slight improvement the following season but then another slump in 1990 and 1991 with nothing on the scoreboard, the team's already beleaguered budget hammered to death when one driver wrote off no fewer than eleven chassis during a single season.

You could tell how badly things were going when the team's long-suffering press officer could find no enthusiasm within the team to issue a release at the close of business on a particularly disappointing race day – of which there were many. Mind you, on the rare occasions when things went well, the state of euphoria within the motorhome would also rule out the desire to fiddle about with producing a press release. Everyone knew they had achieved a decent result – so why bother? It was hard to argue with such straightforward logic as the cognac flowed from Guy Ligier's generous hand.

There was an upturn in 1992 when a new factory was opened at Magny-Cours

There was an upturn in 1992 when a new factory was opened at Magny-Cours. With the modern facility backing on to the venue for the French Grand Prix, Ligier effectively had his personal test track. He also had Renault engines. But no results. A major shake-up followed when the team was taken over by Cyril de Rouvre, a French businessman who took the controversial step of hiring two hard-charging Britons, Mark Blundell and Martin Brundle. There was outrage in France over the hiring of 'Les Rosbifs' but de Rouvre explained there was no one more suitable to be found at home. The British boys supported his claim by scoring a handful of third places and giving Ligier fifth place in the Constructors' Championship. The new lease of life had brought decent results. Once again, Ligier appeared to be the great untapped source of potential. De Rouvre had passed Go. But he also went to jail for various misdemeanours outside motor racing.

Ligier therefore entered 1994 in a state of uncertainty, although with continued support from Gitanes and the national lottery company, Loto, the team was a going concern. By July Flavio Briatore, boss of the Benetton team, had bought into Ligier. Guy Ligier, no longer interested enough to attend the races, continued to hold 15 per cent of the shares. Briatore placed his engineering director at Benetton, Tom Walkinshaw, in charge of turning the team around.

It was a considerable challenge for the no-nonsense Scotsman since he was responsible for the merging of several different cultures: French (Ligier), British (the Walkinshaw way of doing things) and Japanese (Mugen-Honda supplying the engines in 1995). Walkinshaw got so far in his campaign but then reached the point where, in order to have the team working exactly as he wanted, it would be necessary to take complete control.

Briatore was interested in selling but Guy Ligier, perhaps predictably, asked an impossible price for his shares and generally seemed to prevaricate. In the end, Walkinshaw walked away from the team, taking some of the engineering staff with him.

This was at the start of the 1996 season. Ligier's future appeared limited – just as it always had done. Then, defying all predictions once more, the French team won the most prestigious race of the lot, the Monaco Grand Prix.

It was an excellent victory. Olivier Panis, who had finished more races than any other driver in 1994 and then suffered a lack-lustre season the next year, drove the race of his life. He was helped by a car which was perfect on the day, and team tactics which worked brilliantly as the early rain ceased and the track dried out.

Running in seventh place, Panis had actually overtaken a few cars and he was carefully examining the drying track, waiting for the right moment to change from wet tyres to slicks. At any other circuit, a premature change would not have been such a risk since there would have been room for error. At Monaco, as Michael Schumacher had proved on the opening lap, an inch out of line, even at 50 m.p.h., means damage to machinery and pride.

At the end of his twenty-seventh lap, Heinz-Harald Frentzen, who had been running at the back of the field following an earlier indiscretion, felt he had nothing to lose by making what seemed like an early change to dry-weather tyres. His subsequent pace would indicate the folly or otherwise of the decision, proof coming from the TAG-Heuer monitor as the Sauber driver's lap time was thrown up on the screen. Paulo Cattani, Panis's engineer, was not prepared to wait that long.

The monitor, on another page, also showed each lap in progress, split times breaking it into three parts. When Cattani noted that Frentzen had covered the middle section three seconds faster than anyone else, he did not to wait to see the lap completed and called Panis in immediately. That action alone would be worth several seconds and a couple of places.

David Coulthard had been 3.8 seconds and three places ahead of the Ligier as Panis dived into the pits. By the time the McLaren driver had taken his turn, a full two laps later, he emerged 6 seconds behind the Ligier – and this despite a faster stop by Coulthard's crew. The Scotsman chased Panis to the flag but the evidence suggested that McLaren had thrown away their first victory since 1993. Why did they wait so long to bring in Coulthard?

There was another element which needed careful consideration. Had the wet conditions evident at the start continued throughout the race, the reduced speed of the cars would have meant that most could have made it to the finish without the need to refuel.

Gauloises: long-time supporters of Ligier ▶

But as the lap times fell, it became clear that additional fuel would be needed. Just how much, and when, was the crucial factor.

By bringing in a car at the same time as Panis and topping up the tank, would that be sufficient to complete the final two-thirds distance? If not, and another quick stop was required a few laps from the end, would it not be more sensible to complete those laps now, then change tyres and refuel in the knowledge that the driver would be able to run non-stop to the flag?

It was a desperately difficult decision to make. Lap times were falling; fuel consumption was going up; each pit stop would take thirty seconds; the race might be cut short (as, indeed, did happen) if the two-hour mark was reached ahead of the scheduled seventy-eight laps, thus switching the emphasis yet again by reducing the need for fuel. As engineers stabbed their calculators in the midst of this frenzy, drivers were shouting

▲ *After the ball was over. Two weeks after Monaco, Ligier had to be content with sixth place for Pedro Diniz in Spain*

on the radio that the track was drying and they wanted to come in for slicks. Now! It was a team manager's worst nightmare.

Cattani had made an instant decision, arguing that the dramatic reduction in lap times and urgent need for slicks made other factors irrelevant. He was proved correct. He was also lucky. The race was shortened by three laps but, even so, as Panis started his last lap, the Mugen-Honda fuel consumption computer was registering zero. When mechanics tried to restart the Ligier after it had been parked outside the Royal Box, they couldn't. The tank was bone dry.

The Monaco Grand Prix has never been a race as such, more a skilful game of chance, as was demonstrated gloriously by Panis and Ligier. The pit had been manned by a band of Ligier faithfuls and their pleasure was intensified by the failure of both of Flavio Briatore's Benettons, and both cars from Arrows, the team on which Tom Walkinshaw was now lavishing his attention. There was justice after all, and the loyal Jacques Laffite was enjoying the fun more than anyone as he made the most of his role as ambassador for his former employer. The champagne flowed that afternoon. The following morning, the headline in the French national sporting paper, *L'Equipe*, summed up such a crazy Grand Prix: PANIS? INCREDIBLE!

Two weeks later in Spain, Ligier finished a distant sixth. It said everything about this wonderfully erratic inhabitant of the Grand Prix paddock.

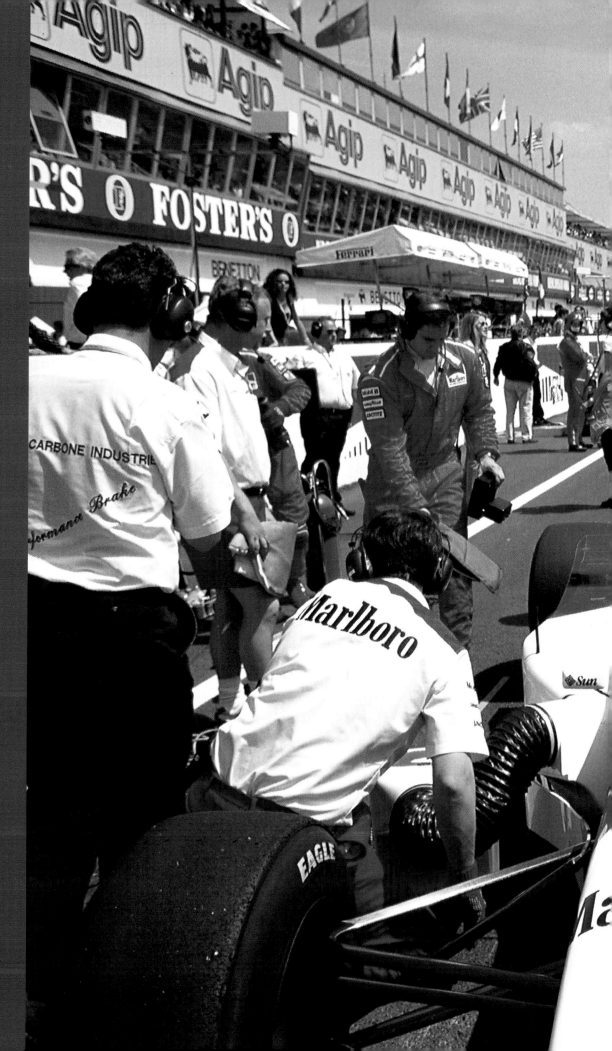

McLAREN

McLAREN

McLAREN

DRIVERS:

MIKA HAKKINEN (FINLAND)

DAVID COULTHARD (SCOTLAND)

TEAM PRINCIPAL • RON DENNIS

CHIEF DESIGNER • NEIL OATLEY

CAR • McLAREN MP4/11

ENGINE • MERCEDES-BENZ V10

FIRST GRAND PRIX • MONACO, 1966

GRANDS PRIX CONTESTED • 427

WINS • 104

It is only natural that today's Formula One teams should bear no relation to their past. The pace of development in Grand Prix racing has been so rapid that any vestige of days gone by is regarded as a sign of failing to keep in touch. It is passé; as old-fashioned as string vests and nylon shirts.

Nowhere is that more evident than at McLaren. The sombre grey efficiency of McLaren International has about as much in common with the founding company – Bruce McLaren Motor Racing – as the boardroom of ICI has with a village chemist. The imperious efficiency of McLaren, the most successful team in Grand Prix racing, would be anathema to the seat-of-the-pants crusading atmosphere created by Bruce McLaren in 1963. It is the same with the present team headquarters. Whereas McLaren International reside in the hum of air-conditioning and the tinkling of ornamental fountains, Bruce McLaren's early racing cars shared a rented shed in New Malden with a grubby road-grader.

There should be no comparison, of course. If Bruce was alive today, he would dismiss the very thought as irrelevant, stupid and time-wasting. He would be thrilled with the success generated by the team bearing his name; intrigued by the complexities of modern motor racing technology. But it is open to debate whether or not he would approve of the way in which Grand Prix racing is conducted.

Bruce McLaren came from an era when sport and business were beginning to merge, with sport calling the tune. The subsequent reversal of roles was inevitable and Bruce would have been the first to recognize that fact. He would probably be bemused but, at the end of the day, the finely tuned sound of a racing engine and the explosive drama on the track would continue to captivate him. He was too much of a dyed-in-the-wool enthusiast for it to be otherwise.

Bruce's love of racing had been sparked by the exploits of his father in New Zealand, even though his first interest as a boy lay in the national preoccupation with playing for the All Blacks. Those hopes were dashed in a terrible way when at the age of nine he contracted Perthes' disease, a seizing-up of his left hip. After months spent in traction and plaster, he emerged with his left leg one and a half inches shorter than his right. With all hope of field sport now banished, Leslie McLaren's efforts to restore an elderly Austin Ulster two-seater sports racing car provided the ideal distraction for his teenage son. As soon as Bruce was old enough to hold a driving licence he not only raced the Austin in local events but developed and improved it. His experiments with that simple little machine would provide the basic groundwork for some of the most magnificent sports racing cars the world has ever seen.

In 1958, New Zealand introduced a 'Driver to Europe' scheme and Bruce's name was

◀◀ Page 118:
New recruits. David Coulthard and race engineer David Brown moved from Williams to McLaren for 1996

Bruce McLaren's early racing cars shared a rented shed in New Malden with a grubby road-grader

▲ *Marlboro's alliance with McLaren came under strain due to a lack of results in the early part of 1996*

on the list of prospective candidates thanks to having progressed beyond the tiny boxlike Austin Ulster. McLaren had graduated to proper racing cars and his promise was such that he eventually won the scholarship which would provide introductions to the leading lights in Formula One.

At the tender age of twenty, Bruce arrived in England and found a room in a pub next door to the Cooper Car Company in Surbiton, Surrey. He bought a Formula Two Cooper, and with the assistance of a mechanic who had travelled with him from New Zealand maintained and raced the car, which was towed around Europe behind a second-hand Ford Zodiac. McLaren's name came to the fore when in August that year he took the Cooper to the German Grand Prix at the Nürburgring. Because of the long and fearsome nature of the fourteen-mile track, this was the one round of the World Championship which allowed Formula Two cars to race with the Formula One machines. McLaren finished fifth overall. That performance, on such a difficult circuit, assured him of a works drive with the Cooper Grand Prix team. The following day, McLaren celebrated his twenty-first birthday. He had come of age in every sense.

Bruce completed his first full season on the Formula One trail in 1959 and at the end of it he won the United States Grand Prix. At twenty-two, he was the youngest driver ever

to achieve such an honour. Life for a Grand Prix star then was nothing like it is today. A victory in the Nineties brings talk of six-figure sums, endorsements to match and a tax haven in Monte Carlo. In 1960, McLaren was still driving his second-hand Morris Minor and sharing a flat in Surbiton.

His circumstances scarcely changed when he became team leader in 1962 following Jack Brabham's departure to design and build his own cars. In fact, if anything the situation got worse. Cooper, having swept all before them by being the first team to cash in on the switch to rear-engined cars in 1959, had begun a decline which threatened to drag Bruce's reputation with it. The thought of running his own team had never really figured in his calculations but matters reached a head at the end of 1963.

During the off-season the Grand Prix teams travelled to Australia and New Zealand for a championship known as the Tasman Series. It was actually a good excuse to avoid the European winter; a laid-back social tour, interrupted each weekend by a motor race. Bruce always liked to do well at home and a change in the regulations gave him a chance to put one over the opposition. It would require building cars to suit but the Cooper company would not play ball. In the end, McLaren decided to convert the Coopers himself. Bruce McLaren Motor Racing Ltd. was born, more as a matter of necessity than anything else. Almost immediately, the desperately harsh side of the sport struck the fledgeling team.

An early season struggle for the once-great McLaren team in 1996 ▶

Bruce had raced in Formula Junior with Timmy Mayer, a likeable and talented young American who would drive the second car in the Tasman Series. Together they got the championship off to a flying start when McLaren won his home Grand Prix for the first time, with Mayer finishing third. Bruce won two more races before moving across to Australia and then on to the final round in Tasmania. During practice on this fast circuit made up of public roads Mayer crashed into a tree and was killed instantly. It was no consolation for Bruce to wrap up the title by finishing second in the race. But tragedy aside, he had got the taste for running his own team.

A series of meetings and chance events would lead Bruce into racing sports cars at a time when it was becoming fashionable to shoehorn powerfully aggressive American V8 motors into nimble little chassis. At first McLaren adapted Cooper sports cars in that shed in New Malden and then began to build his own cars in a tatty workshop behind a shopping centre in Feltham. While all this was going on he was continuing with the Cooper Formula One team, decent results in 1965 being even more difficult to come by than before. When his sports racing car business showed signs of booming with the advent of a money-rich CanAm Series in North America, the link with Cooper was no longer tenable; they parted company amicably at the end of the year. Now McLaren

◀ *A heavy cross to bear.*
David Coulthard carried
the Scottish colours with
great dignity during a
difficult season

could devote his considerable energy to running his sports cars – and a Grand Prix car as well.

In his excellent biography, journalist Eoin Young described McLaren's rather chaotic set-up: 'His own team that November were like one-armed paper-hangers preparing for Formula One and the newly named CanAm sports car series in 1966, as well as a move (to new premises) in Colnbrook. The office door had a sign on it that read "Don't knock – we don't have that sort of time!" and it was almost literally true.'

Young was adequately qualified to write with such authority. A jovial Kiwi, he was a former bank clerk and part-time motor sport reporter for the *Timaru Herald* who had come to Europe as Bruce's secretary. Now he was a director of the company, along with Bruce and his wife, Pat, and Timmy Mayer's brother, Teddy, a lawyer from Pennsylvania.

Plans for the first McLaren Grand Prix car were desperately hit-and-miss by today's standards

Plans for the first McLaren Grand Prix car, sound enough at the time, were desperately hit-and-miss by today's standards. The chassis was state of the art, an interesting mix of balsa wood sandwiched between sheets of aluminium. It was as progressive as they come but, unfortunately, Bruce did not have a decent engine to power it. McLaren had pinned his hopes on an association with Ford (Bruce drove their sports cars at Le Mans) as a means of persuading the American giant to develop a Ford Indycar engine for Formula One. The backing never materialized.

The first Grand Prix of the 1996 season was at Monaco and the McLaren-Ford was taken to the south of France on a trailer, the team's kit stowed in the back of a lumbering American estate-cum-tow car. Thirty years later, the McLaren team took three massive trucks to Monaco, and their engine suppliers, Mercedes-Benz, brought another three support vehicles and enough spare engines to sink a ship. In 1966, there was just one engine. And that was in the back of the racing car.

The Ford V8 was extremely noisy – but very slow. McLaren later experimented with an Italian engine, using it to power into sixth place and score the team's first championship point in the British Grand Prix. Ford did eventually invest in a proper Grand Prix engine, the DFV, but to Bruce's chagrin the V8 was given to Lotus in 1967. It was not until the following year that McLaren got his hands on the Ford. Now his burgeoning team was ready to take on the best.

The cars were painted a distinctive orange colour and Denis Hulme, the 1967 World Champion, had joined his fellow countryman. Bruce and Denny won a non-championship race apiece before setting off for the Grand Prix season, McLaren giving his team its first World Championship victory in Belgium, Hulme following up with wins in Italy and Canada.

McLaren finished the 1968 season second in the Constructors' Championship and there seemed no reason why the team could not bid for the title the following year. In fact there was just one win (Hulme, in the last race of the season in Mexico) and then a drought for almost three years. In the intervening period, the feet would be cut from beneath this hard-working little team.

True to his word, Bruce had pursued success in the lucrative CanAm series. His big orange sports cars were sensational devices, so much so that no else got a look in. Between 1967 and 1969 the CanAm series became known as 'The Bruce and Denny Show' as the New Zealanders dominated almost every race they entered. Such was their confidence that McLaren and Hulme would establish a grid time in the first practice session and then spend the rest of the day by the hotel swimming pool, confident in the knowledge that the likes of Jackie Stewart, John Surtees and Mario Andretti would be unable to get close.

Bruce loved the engineering challenge, particularly when his team moved into another branch of American racing and built cars to compete in the Indianapolis 500. McLaren relished testing since he was one of the few engineers with the capacity to drive quickly enough to sample his ideas at first hand. Goodwood in Sussex was no longer used for racing but the original perimeter track of the wartime airfield was one of Bruce's favourite test venues since it was only an hour's drive from Colnbrook.

Tuesday 2 June 1970 was a typical day. The sports car for the forthcoming CanAm series was ready for testing and Bruce was there to drive it. He had been through the routine many times as he accelerated out of the pits on a warm, sunny morning and completed a number of laps, stopping every now and then for adjustments. Just before 12.30 p.m., he powered onto Lavant Straight where the huge car, with its fins and bellowing Chevrolet V8, would reach 170 m.p.h. in the twinkling of an eye. Going through a flat-out left-hand kink, part of the rear bodywork came adrift. The car went out of control and slammed into an empty marshals' post. Bruce was killed instantly.

McLaren had been the heart and soul of his team. Hulme, the strongest and bravest of men, broke down when he heard the news. The company would carry on, of course; Bruce would have wanted it that way. But outsiders believed that without their guiding light the McLaren name would disappear. In fact the story had hardly started.

Hulme's distress over the loss made severe burns to his hands – received during practice at Indianapolis – seem irrelevant. The pain was acute, but he drove on. For Bruce. Somehow the team struggled through the remainder of the year, Teddy Mayer and Phil Kerr – an old friend of McLaren's from New Zealand – running the show (Eoin Young, unable to see eye to eye with Mayer, had left some time before to pursue a very successful

McLAREN

career in journalism). The team failed to win a Grand Prix for the first time in three years. But they had survived the debilitating loss of their likeable leader.

The next twelve months were not much better, but for 1972 a cosmetic change – in every sense of the expression – saw the start of a revival. A major sponsorship deal with Yardley was heralded by victory for Hulme in South Africa. A few months later the Whit bank holiday weekend brought extraordinary success when a McLaren won the Indianapolis 500 in the USA, Hulme took the laurels in a non-championship Formula One race in England and a young South African by the name of Jody Scheckter gave a McLaren Formula Two car victory in an international meeting at Crystal Palace. Although

▲ *What would Bruce McLaren have made of the latest technology in Formula One?*

McLAREN

the Formula Two programme was eventually scrapped, such a variety of interests was typical of McLaren at the time: the Colnbrook factory was now churning out enough customer cars to fill half the starting grid at each race of the CanAm series – which the works cars continued to dominate.

Scheckter, bullish and hugely talented, eventually graduated to the Formula One team, where he made a big impression – particularly at Silverstone in 1973. As the field rushed through the 170 m.p.h. Woodcote corner at the end of the first lap of the British Grand Prix, Scheckter lost control of his car. The Yardley McLaren shot across the front of the pursuing pack, and as it nudged the pit wall on the inside of the track it seemed Scheckter might have got away with such a fundamental mistake. Then he rolled back just enough to collect another car, and suddenly all hell had broken loose. Nine drivers were involved in the ensuing carnage. Luckily, injuries were limited to one broken ankle. Scheckter escaped unhurt although one owner, having witnessed the wipe-out of his entire team, wished to do the McLaren driver considerable harm.

Scheckter was snapped up by the Tyrrell team for 1974, by which time McLaren had moved into an important new phase by signing a deal with Philip Morris. The association with the Marlboro brand exists to this day in one of the longest-running sponsorship arrangements in world sport. Emerson Fittipaldi, the 1971 World Champion, had joined Hulme. A third car, retaining the Yardley colours, was run for former motorcycle champion Mike Hailwood.

This would be McLaren's ninth season in Grand Prix racing and they had yet to win the constructors' title. Fittipaldi put that right in the process of winning three races and becoming World Champion for the second time. Denis Hulme, such a stalwart of the team, slipped quietly away from the final race of the season and retired without fuss or ceremony to New Zealand. His place was taken by the young German driver Jochen Mass.

Although Fittipaldi won the opening Grand Prix of the 1975 season in Argentina, he was prevented from scoring the double thanks to a turn-around in fortunes for Ferrari. Emerson finished second in the championship to Niki Lauda but delayed signing again for McLaren. By the time Fittipaldi had decided to throw in his lot with an all-Brazilian team run by his brother, it was 22 November and desperately late in the day for Teddy Mayer to find a suitable replacement. As luck would have it, however, this would be the catalyst for one of the most dynamic partnerships in the early history of the team. Within thirty-six hours, Mayer had signed James Hunt.

The renegade Englishman had just been made redundant by the closure of the cash-strapped Hesketh team. The McLaren deal was a marriage of convenience and, in truth,

Nine drivers were involved in the ensuing carnage

many observers felt the liaison was bound to end in tears. In fact the relationship, while rumbustious at times, gelled just as impressively as the new-found maturity in Hunt's driving. In a topsy-turvy season of disqualifications, incidents, a fearsome crash involving Hunt's closest rival, Lauda, and a reasonably friendly needle match between the two, Hunt emerged from the final race as World Champion by a single point. Three-quarters of the way through the season the title had seemed a lost cause, but thanks to a couple of brilliantly aggressive drives Hunt had clawed his way back into contention. He was on top of the world. It was only a minor detail that McLaren had lost the Constructors' Championship to Ferrari. Never mind: there was always next season. In fact, it would take several years for McLaren to return as a major force.

You had to read between the lines to see the start of the regression in 1977. Hunt won three Grands Prix; he was actually driving better than ever. The problem was it took half of the season to make the latest car truly competitive, and in the background the very members of the British media who had raised James high on a pedestal twelve months before were busy knocking him off it. Mind you, the carefree Hunt did provide ample ammunition, most noticeably in Canada where he collided with his team-mate, Mass, and then felled a marshal who came to his aid. Hunt's victory in Japan, the final race of the season, would be his last.

His motivation plummeted in direct proportion to the growing uncompetitiveness of the car. By the end of 1978, a year in which he either crashed, retired or finished outside the top four, James had decided to leave, his place being taken by the hapless John Watson. In a crass piece of image-making, Marlboro tried to shape the gentle Ulsterman into the next James Hunt. It was an embarrassing failure, made worse by the 1979 McLaren being woefully uncompetitive. Watson was a gifted driver but not even his natural talent could urge the cumbersome car into respectability. McLaren even resorted to spending £100,000 on designing and building a completely new car halfway through the season. It was hardly worth the bother.

Somehow Watson managed to persevere, but his position was made even more uncomfortable in 1980 when Mayer signed a diminutive youngster called Alain Prost – who promptly proved faster than his more experienced team-mate. It didn't really matter which of the two drivers was the quicker; neither of them was achieving much as the McLaren name sunk lower into the mire.

Philip Morris had seen enough. Mayer was 'encouraged' to join forces with Project Four Racing Ltd., a thrusting young company with a former mechanic at its helm. This was to be Ron Dennis's passport into Formula One and a decade of exceptional achievement.

Hunt's victory in Japan, the final race of the season, would be his last

At eighteen, Dennis had earned his place as mechanic for the Cooper Formula One team in 1966, then moved to Brabham. Tiring of working for someone else, he set up a Formula Two team in 1971. By the end of the decade he had built up a fine reputation for immaculate preparation and professional presentation, his company, Project Four (in deference to the number of different projects he had been involved in along the way) setting new standards in various junior formulas. Now Dennis wanted to take the logical step into Formula One.

First he had to find a top-rate designer not already engaged in Grand Prix racing. John Barnard was talented and ambitious and Dennis got the Englishman's attention by saying he would have a free hand at the drawing board. Barnard suggested a chassis built entirely from carbon fibre. It would be light and strong. But it had never been done before. And it would not be cheap. Dennis, trusting Barnard's judgement implicitly, said he would somehow find the money and put a team together.

Walking straight into Formula One and setting up shop was a possibility – but it would be very difficult. The answer was a merger with McLaren: on the one hand, a great team struggling to maintain its dignity; on the other, an enterprising newcomer with a daring project on the drawing board. On 1 November 1980, McLaren International came into being.

McLAREN

With Prost lured to the Renault team for the honour of France and all that, the drivers would be John Watson and the Italian Andrea de Cesaris. Philip Morris, now satisfied that the McLaren name was on the road to recovery, would continue to be the major sponsor. Teddy Mayer would stay on as a director. Tyler Alexander, who had started as a mechanic with Bruce during his first forays into sports car racing in America, would remain a shareholder.

The carbon-fibre McLaren (designated MP4, to represent Marlboro-Project Four) was not ready until the fourth race of the 1981 season. Barnard's design looked every inch a winner but there were dark comments from rival engineers. Carbon fibre was undoubtedly strong and light but there was uncertainty over how it would perform in the event of a crash, particularly if the car had more than one impact during the course of its collision. No one, especially Dennis and Barnard, was about to risk their drivers unnecessarily. But the nagging doubt remained.

In the event, the erratic ways of de Cesaris (cruelly nicknamed de Crasheris by the Formula One paddock) provided a more than adequate tribute to the integrity of the McLaren chassis. Indeed rivals soon changed their tune when Watson began to move the red and white car further up the grid at each successive race. Then he finished third in Spain and second in France. The next Grand Prix would be the British. Could Watson win at home?

In the early stages of the race, the answer seemed to be in the negative. He had narrowly missed a pile-up in the opening laps (typically, de Cesaris had shot straight into the mêlée) and dropped to a distant ninth place. Watson put his head down and went motoring, gradually moving up the order, either through neat passing moves or after the misfortunes of others. Suddenly he was third. Then second. When the leading Renault slowed with engine trouble seven laps from the finish Watson could scarcely believe his luck. As he crossed the line and took the flag, the Ulsterman received a tumultuous welcome. It was the most popular victory at Silverstone in years. Luck may have entered into it, but it was perfectly clear that McLaren had turned the corner. Dennis, meanwhile, was looking further down the road.

De Cesaris's future, never secure at the best of times, was definitely in peril when he crashed so often during practice for the Austrian Grand Prix that he reduced his long-suffering mechanics to total despair. Searching for a star name, Dennis and Marlboro pulled off a major coup when they persuaded Niki Lauda, who had retired at the end of 1979, to make a return. It was a brave and brilliant move by both sides.

Lauda won the third race of his comeback in 1982 with a demonstration of his familiar speed and calm precision. It was as if he had never been away. Watson,

meanwhile, was quietly gathering enough points, thanks in part to wins in Belgium and Detroit, to run for the championship. He needed to win the final round in Las Vegas, and after a disappointing practice he stormed through the field to finish second. It was typical of John's career: so near and yet so far, another story of what might have been.

For Ron Dennis and John Barnard, it was a case of knowing exactly what they wanted to happen next. It was time for Teddy Mayer and the intensely loyal Tyler Alexander to stand aside. In December 1982, Dennis bought them out of the business they had helped establish. Barring one or two mechanics there was none of the old guard left, although Alexander would later return in a key managerial role.

Dennis talked about his team being consistently successful, winning more than five Grands Prix in a season. It was not an idle dream. To raise his game, Dennis knew McLaren would need to switch to a turbocharged engine and, typically, neither he nor Barnard was satisfied with anything that was available off the shelf. So Dennis commissioned Porsche to build an engine to Barnard's specification on the understanding that McLaren would raise the finance.

Dennis turned to Mansour Ojjeh, whose family ran Techniques d'Avant Garde (TAG), a Saudi-connected high-technology trading company which was co-sponsoring the Williams team. It would be a major step forward for TAG. Ojjeh moved on from Williams and established TAG Turbo Engines, an independent company which would handle the engine built by Porsche.

The first McLaren TAG-Porsche appeared in August 1983. And not before time. Three months previously, McLaren had suffered the total ignominy of failing to qualify either car for the Monaco Grand Prix. In front of such a high-rolling and influential audience, Dennis could only talk of the future. This was a transitional season, McLaren finishing fifth in the Constructors' Championship. But 1984 would be a different story.

Unfortunately for John Watson, he would not be a part of it. A clumsy attempt to hold out for a higher salary backfired when Prost suddenly became available after unexpectedly parting company with Renault. Dennis and Marlboro welcomed the Frenchman with open arms, leaving Watson out in the cold. With a partnership of Lauda and Prost at the wheel, and the TAG-Porsche engine to power Barnard's latest creation, McLaren was ready.

Prost laid down a marker with victory in the opening Grand Prix in Brazil. Between them Prost and Lauda won twelve of the season's sixteen races, the veteran Austrian pipping Prost by just half a point at the final round. But Lauda was the first to admit that Prost had generally been the faster driver of the two. The McLaren TAG-Porsche had been the car to beat. The Frenchman's turn would surely come.

For Ron Dennis and John Barnard, it was a case of knowing exactly what they wanted

In fact Lauda won just one race in 1985, Prost's tally of five victories being enough to give him the title before the season had finished. McLaren were Constructors' Champions for the second year running, and on that note Lauda decided to end a distinguished career by retiring once again to concentrate on his commercial airline.

Lauda was replaced by Keke Rosberg but the 1982 World Champion could not prove a match for Prost. Both drivers had a fight on their hands thanks to a surge by the Williams team, courtesy of the Honda turbo powering Nigel Mansell and Nelson Piquet. While the two Williams drivers fought it out, taking points from each other as well as everyone else, Prost, to his great surprise, cruised through the middle at the last race and won the driver's title for the second year in succession. Williams and Honda made absolutely sure of the championship in 1987, by which time Ron Dennis was advancing his plans for the next important development by McLaren International.

In the light of developments over the previous couple of seasons (including the departure of John Barnard), if Dennis's master plan was to continue then there were two things he would need: Honda power and the services of Ayrton Senna. In typical Dennis style, he got them both. The TAG-Porsche era had yielded twenty-five wins from

◀ **McLaren spent 1996
searching for a place
in the sun**

sixty-eight races, an excellent record by any standard. But those figures were about to be blown apart in a phenomenally successful season in 1988.

McLaren-Hondas won fifteen out of the sixteen races. They might have had a full set had Senna not tripped over a back-marker while leading at Monza. It was an unbelievable achievement but, as with all good things, there had to be a downside, even if it was not evident at the time.

Prost and Senna were unquestionably the best drivers of the day, albeit different in style and temperament. Whereas Ayrton was the faster – but not by much – Alain was the better racer, a crafty campaigner with a deceptively smooth approach in the cockpit. As Senna found his feet, Prost discovered that his team-mate was gradually taking control of the team which had been his own personal domain for so long. Senna won the championship in 1988, but the following year the rivalry between the two grew in intensity, coming to a head at the penultimate race in Japan. Once again, the McLaren-Hondas were in a league of their own. On this occasion Prost truly had the measure of Senna, and tiring of the Brazilian's intimidatory tactics, simply bundled his team-mate off the road as Senna tried to force his way into the lead. By so doing, Prost effectively won the world title.

Senna was incensed and carried his grudge into 1990, even though Prost had left to join Ferrari. With Gerhard Berger as his team-mate, Senna effectively had McLaren to

himself. The trouble was, he wanted control of everything else as well. With the championship boiling down to another battle between Prost and Senna, the boot was on the other foot this time, with Senna having the points advantage. Going into the first corner of the penultimate round – once again, in Japan – Senna rammed the back of the Ferrari and took both cars out of the race to become World Champion. When Ron Dennis supported his driver's tactics, it raised the suggestion that while Dennis may have been running the team Senna was calling the important shots. But whatever the interpretation, McLaren had won the Constructors' Championship for a sixth time. Meanwhile, another legacy of the earlier domination was beginning to show its head.

It was towards the close of that remarkable season in 1988 that Dennis had decided to build the ultimate road car, a fascinating engineering project but a financial folly given that the idea was conceived at a time of boom and reached metal as the market was spiralling towards bust. Dennis, in association with TAG Group which now owned 60 per cent of McLaren, had also expanded McLaren's industrial base by establishing a marketing company, TAG Electronics, and a Land Speed Record project, as well as pursuing a site in Kent for a test track and a business park in which to base the burgeoning TAG-McLaren Group.

Formula One: the core business of the TAG-McLaren Group ▶

◀ *Mika Hakkinen:*
McLaren driver since
1993

138 **McLAREN**

Grand Prix rivals rubbed their hands in the belief that Dennis had taken his eye off the Formula One ball. Such criticism smacked of sour grapes; Dennis's success, and his sometimes simplistic attitude, had generated considerable envy in the Formula One paddock. In any case, there was no end to the roll of honour as Senna won another driver's championship in 1991, giving McLaren their seventh constructors' title. Then the gravy train began to head towards the buffers. At the end of 1992, Honda withdrew. It caught Dennis, a man who put great store by his ability to plan years ahead, very much by surprise.

A late deal was completed for use of the Ford engine, but purely on a customer basis. Nonetheless, Dennis still had an ace card in Senna and the Brazilian proved it with one or two superlative victories in an increasingly competitive car, in particular a win at the last race of the season in Australia to give McLaren their 104th victory, a record at the time.

McLaren began to thrash around, switching engine suppliers in three successive seasons

Then Senna, unsettled ever since the departure of Honda, dared to leave the team and join McLaren's great rival, Williams. The subtext was that despite the strength of the personal relationship between Dennis and the great Brazilian, McLaren were no longer capable of providing a winning car. It was almost a personal affront to Ron Dennis. Without either Senna or Honda, McLaren began to thrash around, switching engine suppliers in three successive seasons and, for the first time since 1984, going racing without a World Champion on their books. It did indeed seem as though Dennis had dropped the ball some time before.

For 1995, a deal with Mercedes-Benz seemed certain to stop the rot, but in fact the team reached a new low when Marlboro, searching for a star name, prompted Dennis to sign Nigel Mansell, then in serious decline. The liaison lasted until May of that year, by which time McLaren had become a laughing stock after it had been revealed that Mansell did not fit the cockpit of the latest car. Dennis stoically insisted that he would apply his tried and proven methods and turn the team around. It took more than a year, but after three difficult races at the beginning of 1996, his persistence and patience began to pay off.

The team had not deserved the ignominy of such a miserable phase. Throughout their troubles, the personnel, immaculately turned out as ever, had performed with quiet professionalism and dignity, the standards of excellence instilled by Dennis always to the fore. McLaren's resurgence was well received within Formula One. But only because it was good for business. Ever since McLaren became a grey monolith more than a decade ago, there has been tremendous respect, but very little affection for the team. That died at Goodwood on 2 June 1970.

MINARDI

 MINARDI

MINARDI

DRIVERS:

PEDRO LAMY (PORTUGAL)

GIANCARLO FISICHELLA (ITALY)

TARSO MARQUES (BRAZIL)

TEAM PRINCIPAL • GIANCARLO MINARDI

CHIEF DESIGNER • GABRIELE TREDOZI

CAR • MINARDI M195B

ENGINE • FORD V8

FIRST GRAND PRIX • BRAZIL, 1985

GRANDS PRIX CONTESTED • 172

WINS • 0

There is the story about the coffee machine at the Minardi motorhome. One day it broke down and the paddock came close to panic. More Minardi mechanics were spotted working on it than had ever been seen labouring on the cars. Even Giancarlo Minardi himself lent a hand during this time of crisis. All was soon made good and the thick black coffee began to pour once again. Calm returned to this unobtrusive corner of the Formula One world.

Minardi's coffee is excellent. So too is the pasta. But it's not so much the quality which matters; it's the warmth of the welcome and the absence of pretension. It is not an exaggeration to say that Minardi is the best-liked team in the paddock. And that depth of feeling is not merely confined to Italians shunned by the political mayhem at Ferrari; the respect for what Giancarlo Minardi is trying to achieve – and the way he does it – is universal.

Minardi are never likely to win a Grand Prix, unless by fluke, and it is that paradoxical love of the underdog – as healthy in Grand Prix racing as in any other sport – which makes them so popular. If they managed to find lasting competitiveness and regularly challenged the established front runners, attitudes would doubtless change. But as things stand there is a massive closet Minardi fan club in the paddock. On the rare occasions when the little team scores a championship point or two, most of the pit lane rejoices for them.

Giancarlo Minardi may not agree with this view, but his team retain the image of a happy privateer attempting to take on the million-dollar Goliath. The good and the great of Grand Prix racing generally have no time for waifs and strays but the Minardi team, having battled for more than ten years, are an integral part of the scene. It will be a very sad day if they are ever forced to leave. Giancarlo Minardi himself would be like a lost soul. Racing is in his blood.

The Minardi family runs the oldest Fiat dealership in Italy. Established by Guiseppe Minardi and his two brothers in Faenza in 1927, the company was later run by Giancarlo's father, Giovanni, who died tragically during surgery when Giancarlo was thirteen. Giovanni's wife, Elena, a remarkable lady by all accounts, took charge until Giancarlo and his two younger brothers were old enough to assume control in the early 1970s. Eventually each found his own niche, Guiseppe running the Fiat dealership, Nando taking charge of the Iveco truck business, and Giancarlo concentrating on the racing team.

Giancarlo had raced briefly at club level before deciding that his talents lay in management rather than driving. In 1972 he took charge of Scuderia del Passatore, a team named after a Robin Hood figure in Romagna and racing in Italian formulas. The name changed to Scuderia Everest in 1974, thanks to substantial backing from the

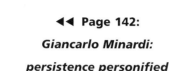

◄◄ Page 142:
*Giancarlo Minardi:
persistence personified*

**Minardi are never
likely to win a Grand
Prix, unless by fluke**

MINARDI

Everest accessories firm which allowed the team to move into the European Formula Two Championship. This lasted for six years, the little outright success they had being no match for the fun Minardi derived from his team. In order to progress, however, Minardi felt it would be necessary to build his own cars rather than race off-the-shelf customer versions. Scuderia Minardi was formed at the end of 1979.

The team was established by Giancarlo Minardi, Pietro Mancini (a well-known and reasonably well-heeled figure in Italian motor racing circles) and Giacomo Caliri, a former engineer with Ferrari who had established the FLY design studio, from where the drawings of the first Minardi racing car soon emerged.

Minardi chose to continue in Formula Two and the first year, 1980, was spent dealing with the inevitable teething problems. In 1981, however, Minardi signed Michele Alboreto, a promising young driver who went on to win Grands Prix for Ferrari and

MINARDI

Tyrrell. The Italian gave Minardi his first victory that year, and when he moved on to higher ground, Giancarlo made another shrewd move by signing Alessandro Nannini, a protégé of Mancini and a likeable, carefree driver who would play a key part in Minardi's affairs during the next few seasons. Nannini produced some impressive drives, as did another new driver, Pierluigi Martini, who became a cornerstone of the Formula One effort.

Giancarlo Minardi had been thinking about Grand Prix racing, particularly since in 1985 Formula Two was about to make way for Formula 3000, an alternative which was unlikely to raise enthusiasm among prospective sponsors. However, the need to have a turbocharged engine to be competitive in Formula One would prove an expensive stumbling block – assuming Minardi could find a manufacturer willing to sell him one in the first place. Negotiations had been conducted with Alfa Romeo and the team got as far as testing an Alfa turbo in the back of a converted Formula Two car. Then the motor company withdrew their consent.

The only way round the supply problem was to have one built. In 1984 Minardi persuaded Carlo Chiti, a venerated engineer with Alfa Romeo, to leave and design a turbo engine to be known as the Motori Moderni. Minardi Team S.p.A. was now set to go Grand Prix racing. Or so they thought.

Despite working flat out, Chiti's engine was not ready for the start of the 1985 Formula One season, Minardi having to make do with a non-turbocharged Ford-Cosworth engine. That drawback was understandable enough. Not so easy to comprehend was a decision by the sport's governing body not to grant Nannini the necessary licence to go racing in Formula One, on the grounds that he did not have enough experience. Martini drove the single Minardi entry until such time as Nannini had the necessary qualifications.

In fact, Nannini did not miss much in 1985. The Motori Moderni V6 arrived in time for the third race and was immediately uncompetitive, the team suffering from a string of engine problems. Results were so poor that Martini's confidence and reputation were shot to pieces and he went off to race in Formula 3000.

Nannini had the correct paperwork for 1986 but the authorities had done him no favours. The Minardi-Motori Moderni continued to be a liability, and not even a switch in 1987 from the uncompetitive Pirelli tyres used thus far to Goodyear redeemed a hopeless situation. The turbo was underpowered and excessively thirsty, and on one occasion during practice in Detroit in 1987 matters had got so bad that when his engine failed yet again and stranded him out on the circuit Nannini didn't bother to go back to the Minardi pit. He returned instead to his nearby hotel, where he showered and changed before facing Giancarlo's temporary wrath over his insouciance. He was missed at Minardi, where he could frequently be found, cigarette in one hand, cup of powerful espresso coffee in the other, but during the course of his struggles he had done enough to attract the attention of Benetton.

As had become the norm, both cars retired from that race, but a year later the punishing street circuit gave Minardi their first milestone. Having finally abandoned the Motori Moderni, a switch had been made to the more reliable Ford V8. For the first half of the season two Spaniards, Luis Sala and Adrian Campos, drove for the team but after a failure to qualify for three races in succession Campos was shown the door and Martini, who had given a good account of himself in Formula 3000, was recalled for the Detroit Grand Prix. It was a glorious return. Not only did he qualify comfortably, he finished sixth to give the team their first championship point.

Caliri left the team soon after and Minardi gambled by hiring Aldo Costa, a twenty-seven-year-old engineer not long out of university, and made him technical director. The neat and efficient M189 Minardi-Ford, which arrived four races into the 1989 season, demonstrated that this was another shrewd move by the team owner.

It took a short while for the team to extract the most from the new car, but come the British Grand Prix at Silverstone they were on the pace. Martini finished fifth, and by beating off a late challenge to take sixth place, Sala contributed to a three-point total which elevated Minardi from the ranks of the also-ran and saved them the desperate hassle of having to continue prequalifying at each succeeding race. It was the team's finest hour. Giancarlo and his boys were delirious, the humble Minardi motorhome receiving all manner of visitors keen to express their delight.

That was not all. The team flew home to Italy that night on the same plane as the Ferrari crew. Nigel Mansell's Ferrari had finished second and a rowdy crowd of race fans was waiting at Bologna airport. But they had not come to celebrate Ferrari's result. To the amazement of the Minardi team, it was their achievement which had prompted this outburst of joy.

Riding a crest of a small wave, the Minardis, now enjoying the benefit of Pirelli tyres which were a match for the competition, rattled off a series of top-half-of-the-grid positions. Martini put his car on the third row at Estoril in September and then caused a sensation by briefly leading the Portuguese Grand Prix before eventually finishing fifth. Everyone was thrilled for the happy-go-lucky band of racers which had memorably been referred to in one publication as the 'team from the garage next door'. That summed them up. Minardi Team were a handful of 'good blokes' doing a fine job on hardly any money. If only they could find decent backing, or perhaps secure a works engine.

It was the team's finest hour: Giancarlo and his boys were delirious

▲ Still searching for the promise shown in 1989

The following April, Minardi was just as surprised as everyone else when he achieved the seemingly impossible. It was announced that for 1991 Minardi would have use of Ferrari engines. It was like having Eric Cantona agree to play for Wigan Athletic.

The link between the two companies was not as daft as it seemed. In 1976, Scuderia Everest had been loaned a Ferrari Grand Prix car from the previous year. The intention was to run the car in two non-championship races in England but the arrangement did not come to much, particularly when the driver, Giancarlo Martini (Pierluigi's uncle), crashed the car while on his way to the grid for the first race, and finished a distant tenth in the other. Despite the disappointment, Ferrari had supplied engines for Minardi's Formula Two effort.

This latest development was therefore not new and had a lot to do with the fact that Ferrari was now owned by Fiat, the Minardi garage being a major player in the Fiat dealer network. It seemed the good times were finally about to roll.

Without warning, expected sponsorship from the Pioneer group suddenly switched to Ferrari. Minardi started the 1991 season on the wrong financial foot but Martini nevertheless managed to collect two fourth places. The season was not working out as well as had been expected and the team was undergoing change. Mancini had ended his involvement some time before, and at the end of 1991 Martini quit to join a rival. Tommaso Carletti, a key technician, left for pastures new. Even more disappointing, perhaps, it was decided that the Ferrari engine should go to Dallara, a rival team with which Minardi would eventually merge to allow both outfits to ride out the recession.

During successive years, engines and drivers have been chopped and changed – Alboreto and Martini returning to more or less end their Formula One careers – but a place on the podium seems as far away as ever. The crushing absence of substantial funding and a decent works engine means the chances of running consistently with the top four or five teams remain nothing more than a dream. But it costs nothing to dream.

▲ **The Italian driver Giancarlo Fisichella showed impressive form in 1996**

The Minardi team, numbering no more than eighty people, is made up of enthusiasts who adore their motor racing. The family atmosphere remains just as strong as it did when several years ago the entire team travelled to the Spanish Grand Prix in two minibuses, one driven by Tommaso Carletti and the other by Alessandro Nannini. Such things may be sneered at by loftier rivals with their private jets and first-class travel, but for many enthusiasts around the world Minardi is the essence of a deep love of the sport.

Supporters of the Italian team can be found in the most unlikely places – such as a small village in rural Sussex. The West Lavington Association of Minardi Enthusiasts is run by Geoff Willis, an executive with a major pharmaceutical-cum-crop-protection company. Willis and like-minded fans of the team formed the club because they admired the efforts of Giancarlo Minardi and liked the open and friendly style of his team. Willis wrote: 'I have been overwhelmed by the way in which the project has been received and by the willingness of people to be helpful, not least Minardi themselves.' As a means of keeping members scattered across the world informed and united, the association produces a club magazine, an immaculately presented document oozing enthusiasm of the kind on which the team itself thrives.

Minardi's policy of giving young talent a chance (assuming the backing could be found) led to promising outings by the Brazilian Tarso Marques in 1996 ▶

 MINARDI

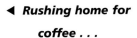

Despite the many trials and tribulations faced by Scuderia Minardi, the sense of fun is never far from the surface. In one issue of the supporters' magazine, an interview with Pierluigi Martini had been reproduced. In a world where racing drivers tend to take themselves far too seriously, Martini's answer to the final question makes refreshing reading and sums up life at Minardi.

When asked which three items he would like if stranded on a desert island, Martini replied: 'Water, Claudia Schiffer and a telephone – to inform everyone that I am with her.' The only surprise is that he didn't mention Minardi's famous coffee machine.

◄ *Rushing home for*

coffee . . .

SAUBER

SAUBER

SAUBER

DRIVERS:

HEINZ-HARALD FRENTZEN (GERMANY)

JOHNNY HERBERT (ENGLAND)

TEAM PRINCIPAL • PETER SAUBER

CHIEF DESIGNER • LEO RESS

CAR • SAUBER C15

ENGINE • FORD V10

FIRST GRAND PRIX • SOUTH AFRICA, 1993

GRANDS PRIX CONTESTED • 48

WINS • 0

Switzerland and motor racing have been uncomfortable bedfellows ever since 11 June 1955. On that day, a Mercedes-Benz sports car flew into a section of the crowd watching the opening stages of the Le Mans twenty-four-hour race. Eighty people were killed. The Mercedes-Benz and its driver, Pierre Levegh, had nothing to do with Switzerland. The race itself was in France. But the shocking accident was enough to have international motor racing banned from Switzerland, a law which holds to this day.

The irony is that a road circuit at Berne had been considered one of the best of its kind in the early Fifties. It was fast and challenging but the authorities were uneasy about staging the Swiss Grand Prix on such a potentially hazardous track. The Le Mans tragedy was the excuse they had been waiting for. The continuing ban is typical, in the eyes of more adventurous folk, of a beautiful and clinically correct country which has very little else to say for itself.

Establishing a motor racing team within the Swiss borders is therefore a task which does not come easily. There is a small amount of club racing at local level, but significantly there is not the network of specialized industries which, for example, has grown up in every nook and cranny in England during the past fifty years. It would also be unlikely to find a reception in honour of the motor sport business and all it has achieved for the good of the country, as there frequently is at Westminster. A Grand Prix team in Zurich holds about as much official interest as a sumo wrestling club in Wimbledon.

Due credit then to PP Sauber AG, the only Swiss motor sport enterprise to have kicked the traces and performed with honour abroad. Others have tried, and failed immediately. The reason for the success in this instance is due to the vision and persistence of one man: Peter Sauber, a former electrician from Zurich.

Sauber's association with motor racing began when he bought a Volkswagen Beetle from a friend and raced it in Swiss club events in 1967. Because of his training, Sauber discovered that he was fascinated by the technology of racing cars rather than driving them. His engineering talent led to the production of a Beetle-based racing buggy, a strange device which quickly earned the name Cheese Sandwich because of its outrageous appearance. Looks counted for little however when Sauber used it to win the 1969 Formula Racing Car Club Championship. He was well and truly hooked.

Utilizing a Brabham racing car as the basis for his next, more adventurous, project, Sauber designed and built a sports car in the cellar of his parents' home. This would be known, quite simply, as a Sauber C1, the C in recognition of his wife, Christiane. Little did he realize that by the time he reached C14 his cars would be taking on the best in the world.

◄◄ Page 156:
Peter Sauber

A Grand Prix team in Zurich holds about as much official interest as a sumo wrestling club in Wimbledon

▲ *Sauber has moved from Volkswagen Beetles to championship-winning sportscars to Formula One*

Sauber won the Swiss Championship with the C1 and his expertise was such that the next four Sauber sports cars led him to international racing, a Sauber starting the Le Mans twenty-four-hour race for the first time in 1977. The car building ceased due to financial constraints and he earned his money by preparing BMWs for racing, one of his potent machines used by two top drivers, Hans Stuck and Nelson Piquet, to win the Nürburgring thousand-kilometre race, a prestigious event across the German border.

The first serious step towards becoming a major constructor in his own right came in 1982 when he was commissioned to design a new sports car for Le Mans. The Ford-powered car, the C6, received due praise, but the efforts of the team were compromised by a lack of continuity and general teething problems. The C7 Sauber ran a BMW engine, and in 1984 Peter Sauber made important contacts within the Mercedes-Benz organization, then making a tentative return to top-level motor sport.

Sauber had asked if he could use the Mercedes-Benz wind tunnel in order to check out the aerodynamics on his car. The motor manufacturer agreed and, more or less peering over his shoulder, were impressed by the quality of his workmanship and the general organization of the small company. When Sauber suggested that his car should form a test bed for an engine Mercedes-Benz had been using for research, they quickly accepted. It was one thing to read impressive performance figures on the dynamometer, quite another to install the engine in a Sauber and learn about the harsh environment of a racing car. Mercedes-Benz were encouraged by the results and it was agreed to enter a car for Le Mans in 1985. The fact that this would be the thirtieth anniversary of their last visit was not mentioned. But it soon would be.

Night practice was held on the Thursday before the race itself. The previous day, the Sauber had been the second-fastest car on the fearfully long Mulsanne Straight, the C8 reaching 221 m.p.h. Sheer speed was obviously not a problem. Seeking improvements in the handling elsewhere on the lap, adjustments were made to the car. The driver, John Nielsen, was sent out as darkness fell.

Nielsen was not trying particularly hard – 'simply warming myself up' was how he described it – as he reached close to 200 m.p.h on the approach to a gentle rise on the Mulsanne Straight. Without any warning, the car became airborne.

Nielsen said later that the sensation was exactly like taking off in a light aircraft. The Sauber simply climbed into the air and completed two back somersaults before landing on its wheels – with the engine still running. The next thing Nielsen knew was that he had been catapulted into the crash barriers, where, not surprisingly, the car was heavily damaged. Fortunately for the driver, the cockpit area was immensely strong and he emerged unhurt. There was no way the team could continue that weekend and the effect of such an accident – at Le Mans, of all places – on Daimler-Benz, the parent company, can be imagined. It was a matter which received more than fleeting discussion around the boardroom table at company headquarters in Stuttgart.

Sauber, meanwhile, continued to pay for his time in the wind tunnel, a deliberate policy to show an inquisitive motor sport press that Mercedes-Benz was not supporting his team and therefore not returning to racing officially. Nonetheless, the engine boffins were intrigued by the problems created by the sports car racing formula which placed heavy emphasis on fuel efficiency. This was the sort of thing which would benefit the Mercedes production cars enormously as well as presenting an acceptable public relations image. It also had to be borne in mind that Mercedes-Benz's rival BMW had become a trendier symbol of fast road cars; an association with motor racing would do Mercedes-Benz no harm at all.

When Peter Sauber chose to enter a full season of sports car racing in 1986, his campaign had unofficial blessing from Stuttgart. By the end of 1987, Mercedes-Benz had more or less come out of the closet; they would make an official comeback the following year.

Sauber-Mercedes won five out of the ten races in 1988 and finished second to Jaguar in the World Championship. With experience gathered, the silver cars swept the boards for two years running, winning the championship each time and finishing first, second and fifth at Le Mans in 1989.

As part of the programme, Mercedes-Benz had introduced a Junior Team; in effect, a nursery school for young drivers as they learned about all aspects of international racing. Sauber's team handled Michael Schumacher, Karl Wendlinger and Heinz-Harald Frentzen, all of whom would reach Formula One. With sports car racing in decline in 1991, it seemed reasonable to assume that Peter Sauber was about to do the same.

◀◀ *Johnny Herbert,*
a winner at Le Mans,
joined the Sauber
Formula One team
in 1996

SAUBER

◀ **Heinz-Harald Frentzen has stayed loyal to Sauber, the team which gave the German driver his Formula One break**

When Sauber won the last sports car race he entered, at Autopolis in Japan on 27 October 1991, it was widely accepted that Sauber and Mercedes were about to take the final step together. Exactly a month later, Mercedes-Benz announced that they would not be entering Grand Prix racing after all. Sauber would be on his own. That was the official line, anyway.

Mercedes-Benz had invested hugely in Sauber's operation. A brand new four-storey headquarters had been built outside the little town of Hinwil, south-east of Zurich. It was as impressive a facility as any in Formula One, visitors never failing to comment on the massive lift which could carry the team's transporter to every floor, the open-plan concept allowing Sauber – if he felt the need – to have his racing car driven into the heart of the drawing office.

He had gathered together an excellent team. Since it would be a shame to allow its disintegration, and even though none of his permanent staff had experience of Formula One, he decided to take the risk and carry on with his plans to enter Grand Prix racing in 1993. The spectre of the Mercedes-Benz symbol, the three-pointed star, would never be far away.

The black cars carried the logo 'Concept by Mercedes-Benz' on their flanks, a reference to the association which was particularly evident in the ten-cylinder engine built by Ilmor Engineering. Ilmor was, in fact, working under contract to Mercedes-Benz, and even though the engine carried the Sauber symbol on the camshaft covers, it was a Mercedes in all but name. Certainly, the German company would not have been ashamed of events in the first race in South Africa, where Karl Wendlinger qualified tenth and his team-mate, JJ Lehto, took sixth place on the grid. When Lehto went on to finish fifth, Sauber could not believe their luck. Championship points – on merit – first time out. It was as impressive a debut as any team could wish for.

Peter Sauber was the first to realize that Grand Prix racing ought not to be as easy as that. The first season would be relatively kind, the Swiss team collecting twelve points and finishing joint sixth in the Constructors' Championship with Lotus. It was a remarkable achievement, particularly as Sauber had deliberately chosen not to select his staff from the traditional sources within the sport. Instead of having Grand Prix people arrive with preconceived ideas, he wanted his team to use the methods which suited him best. 'That way,' he said, 'whatever the other teams do, we can do better.'

One factor affecting his decision had been the difficulty in obtaining work permits in Switzerland; even key members of the team would have to learn the hard way. Nonetheless, Sauber had caused a minor stir by appointing Carmen Ziegler as team manager, the first time a woman had ever held such a post in Formula One. The striking Ms Ziegler

◀ **Drilling**
for performance.
Adjustments to the
rear diffuser on
the Sauber-Ford

certainly caught the attention of the male-dominated media, and officials were to discover that she was no pushover. Her tenure lasted for just one year (after which she went off to get married, much to the distress of certain members of the aforementioned media) and her place was taken by Max Welti, an agreeable former racing driver who had his work cut out during the forthcoming season. Peter Sauber had been heard to say that on balance he thought it was slightly easier to go Formula One racing than tackle the complexities of sports car racing at Le Mans. He was in for a rude shock. PP Sauber AG would be stressed to the limit in 1994.

In fact, the mood within the team had not been particularly good during the latter half of the previous year thanks to the drivers having little time for each other. The trouble had started at Monaco in May when the two Saubers managed to collide, each driver blaming the other. When the management tended to side with Wendlinger, Lehto knew which way the wind was blowing and it was no surprise when he parted company with the team at the end of the year.

Just when motor racing needed a period of calm, Wendlinger crashed

For 1994, Wendlinger was joined by Frentzen, the pair of them picking up six championship points in the first three races. Wendlinger had finished fourth in the San Marino Grand Prix but in truth the team did not have much heart for celebration following the news that Ayrton Senna had died of injuries received in a crash, this following twenty-four hours after a novice, Roland Ratzenberger, had been killed during practice.

Grand Prix racing was still in a state of some agitation two weeks later when the scene shifted to Monte Carlo. The world's press, keen to investigate the dangers of motor racing and, in many cases, to pontificate on a subject they knew little about, had descended on the principality. Just when motor racing needed a period of calm, Wendlinger crashed and was rushed to hospital in a coma. The people of Grand Prix racing, and Sauber in particular, were stunned by this seemingly endless catalogue of misery. The media went into overdrive.

Wendlinger's accident, during practice on the first day, had seemed harmless enough. He had lost control while braking from 170 m.p.h. to 50 m.p.h. for the chicane leading onto the harbour front. The car had slid sideways into a barrier protecting a traffic island on the inside of the chicane. The impact speed was not particularly high but Wendlinger had been unlucky enough to go in at the one point which was not protected by a water-filled cushion. His helmet is believed to have struck the metal barrier.

Reports of Wendlinger being attended to while lying alongside his car made grim reading in the following day's newspapers. *L'Equipe* carried a full front-page photograph under the heading STOP THIS!. It did nothing for anyone's peace of mind, particularly within the boardroom at Stuttgart, since Mercedes-Benz had officially upgraded their involvement by having their logo on the engine and the bodywork, the latter clearly evident in the accompanying photographs. For a company which was rightly proud of its achievements in automotive safety, this was too close for comfort.

While Wendlinger made a slow recovery, there was embarrassment of a different kind a month later. Sauber had started the season with sponsorship from Broker, a hitherto unknown publishing firm active in the stock market. Broker was due to launch an upmarket lifestyle/economics magazine but the publication had not gone beyond the dummy stage. Worse still, this mystery company had defaulted on its first payment in a four-year contract which was reputed to be worth £10 million per season.

The money never did materialize. Mercedes-Benz never said as much but they made up the shortfall even though a worldwide name with such a sound reputation could have done without being indirectly associated with a scam which made the business pages of German newspapers a month after the horrors of Imola and Monaco.

For several weeks there was no certainty that Wendlinger would survive. Gradually, however, he was brought out of his coma, and by October he was back in the cockpit, carrying out a test session to establish just how fit he might be for racing in 1995. In the meantime, Frentzen had been joined by the veteran driver Andrea de Cesaris, but it was on the young German that Sauber rested the heavy responsibility of seeing them through the rest of this dreadful season.

Despite this being Frentzen's first year in Formula One, he drove impressively, qualifying ten times inside the top ten. He started fourth at Jerez in Spain and ran third for much of the time despite carrying more fuel – and therefore more weight – than the leading lights behind him. He had made such a good impression that he was asked, post Imola, to replace Senna at Williams. It was an opportunity any young driver would kill for but such was Frentzen's loyalty to the team which had given him his Formula One chance that he chose not to desert Peter Sauber in his hour of need.

Sadly, such commendable attitudes were not evident within Mercedes-Benz. During 1994, they fell for the smooth blandishments of the McLaren team and threw in their lot with the former World Champions. Now Sauber really did appear to be in trouble.

The question of engine supply for 1995 was a difficult one. The most obvious candidate was Ford, recently given the heave-ho by Benetton in favour of Renault. Against all odds – and to Peter Sauber's great relief – Ford chose the Swiss team. Life was going to be quite different for the American manufacturer after being on top of the world with Benetton.

It took a while for the Sauber engineers, headed by Leo Ress, to come to terms with the different dimensions of the heavier V8 and, at first, Sauber-Ford were struggling

Despite this being Frentzen's first year in Formula One, he drove impressively

▲ *Frentzen: Sauber's greatest asset*

with the resulting handling problems. As the season wore on, however, Frentzen turned in some very fine performances, culminating in third place in the Italian Grand Prix.

Peter Sauber is nothing if not honourable and, true to his word, he gave Wendlinger the opportunity to prove himself at the beginning and at the end of the season. For a driver so naturally talented as the quiet Austrian, it was heartbreaking to watch the mental struggle as he tried to come to terms with the loss of that indefinable touch which every great driver has. But he had been given more than a fair chance. In between, Jean-Christophe Boullion took Wendlinger's place, the highly touted youngster proving a major disappointment and adding nothing to Sauber's efforts as the team appeared to be losing its grip.

There was fresh optimism for 1996, however, when Ford and their allies Cosworth Engineering unveiled a ten-cylinder engine which they hoped would put them on a par

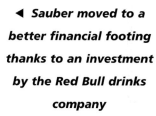

◄ Sauber moved to a better financial footing thanks to an investment by the Red Bull drinks company

with every other engine manufacturer. Red Bull, makers of a powerful 'sports drink', had bought into the team and the final piece in the jigsaw fell into place when Frentzen agreed to stay on and Johnny Herbert, winner of two Grands Prix in 1995, was signed to drive the second car.

The entire package was launched in slightly bizarre circumstances in Switzerland. The set for a musical in a theatre in Baden was chosen to provide a different slant on how new cars should be unveiled, songs and a stage act making strange companions for the stiffly formal speeches. It was an adventurous idea, and yet it seemed out of keeping with the team's rather staid image, as epitomized by Peter Sauber himself. A big man, with a Havana cigar at the ready, he plods quietly through the paddock, rock-steady and unhurried, sidestepping controversy, saying very little. In many ways, just how you would expect a Grand Prix team from Switzerland to be.

TYRRELL

TYRRELL

DRIVERS:

MIKA SALO (FINLAND)

UKYO KATAYAMA (JAPAN)

TEAM PRINCIPAL • KEN TYRRELL

CHIEF DESIGNER • DR HARVEY POSTLETHWAITE

CAR • TYRRELL 024

ENGINE • YAMAHA V10

FIRST GRAND PRIX • SOUTH AFRICA, 1968

GRANDS PRIX CONTESTED • 402

WINS • 33

Ken Tyrrell has been known to berate race organizers abroad for flying the Union flag upside-down. In Ken's book it is not a matter to be taken lightly, and such a response is just what you might expect from an Englishman whose team carries the very British title Tyrrell Racing Organisation. It is also what you might expect from a septuagenarian whose passion for the English cricket team is only marginally less than his love of Grand Prix racing.

Motor sport has lost none of its allure for Ken Tyrrell, despite the fact that his team was at its zenith more than twenty years ago. Ken celebrated his seventy-second birthday at the 1996 San Marino Grand Prix, one of the rare occasions in recent times when the Tyrrell motorhome had a reasonable excuse for breaking out the champagne. Yet despite the absence of success, the Tyrrell team remain a vital part of the Formula One scene, if only because of Ken Tyrrell's bubbling enthusiasm and his stubborn refusal to bow to the advances of the calendar.

Ken Tyrrell knew little about motor racing until he happened across the sport by chance at the age of twenty-seven, and it is almost as if the novelty has never worn off. He refuses to reflect on the 'good old days' but there can be no doubt that the memories created by three world championships with Jackie Stewart have helped sustain the jovial Surrey man during the financially difficult periods – of which there have been many in recent years. And yet the chances are that given the opportunity to do it all again, Tyrrell would choose to follow exactly the same course from the moment he first heard the rasp of a racing engine and sniffed the high-octane air.

The introduction to motor sport came courtesy of football, another Tyrrell passion on a par with cricket. Ken played for the local club in the Surrey village of Ockham and he joined the lads for a coach trip to Silverstone in 1951. It started off as a bit of a jaunt but became a pivotal event which would change his life completely.

Tyrrell loved what he saw and, typically, he waded straight in. Consulting the race programme, he noted that Alan Brown, a driver in the Formula Three race, worked in the motor trade and lived not far from the Tyrrell family home in Guildford. He called unannounced and introduced himself. Brown responded by selling his Cooper single-seater to such a likely punter!

Attacking his new hobby with relish, Tyrrell went motor racing abroad, in between managing the timber business he had established with his brother in Ockham after leaving the Royal Air Force in 1946. Despite winning an international race in Sweden, he was honest enough to realize that he would be better off leaving the driving to someone else while he applied his organizational skills to running a team.

In 1959 he became team manager for the Formula Two team run by the Cooper Car

Page 172:
*Dr Harvey Postlethwaite
(left) and Ken Tyrrell*

**Ken celebrated
his seventy-second
birthday at the
1996 San Marino
Grand Prix**

▲ Mika Salo: another excellent choice by Ken Tyrrell

Company in Surbiton, and a year later he established the Ken Tyrrell Racing Team to run in Formula Junior. Since this category of racing was the only stepping stone to Formula One, Tyrrell dealt with many promising young drivers, one of whom, Henry Taylor, gave the equipe its first international success by winning the prestigious Monaco Junior Grand Prix. By 1963 the team's title had changed to the Tyrrell Racing Organisation. But such stiffly British cosmetic changes aside, the most significant development occurred a year later at the Goodwood racetrack in Sussex.

On the advice of a friend, Tyrrell gave a test drive to a confident young Scotsman by the name of John Young Stewart. Bruce McLaren, then a Grand Prix driver for the Cooper team, established a target time in Tyrrell's Formula Junior car. When Stewart beat

McLaren's efforts with ease, Bruce was sent out again to show the upstart a thing or two. Stewart returned to the cockpit and went faster still. Tyrrell signed the jaunty youngster on the spot.

It was the start of a brilliant partnership, one which earned Tyrrell his reputation as a talent spotter. Ken dismissed the claim in his usual direct fashion. 'If you couldn't see that Jackie was good,' he said, 'then you were an idiot.'

No one disputed Tyrrell's choice when Stewart won the Monaco Formula Three race (Formula Three having replaced Formula Junior) and the British Formula Three Championship. Such was the quality of Stewart's driving that he was offered a place with British Racing Motors, one of the great names in Grand Prix racing at the time. The link with BRM gave Tyrrell access to the Lincolnshire company's Formula Two engine but he had difficulty finding a decent chassis to go with it. The solution would ultimately lead him into Grand Prix racing.

Matra, the French aerospace company, had become involved in the motor manufacturing business and a motor sport policy was seen as the best way of promoting sales of their road cars. Their efforts on the track had met with limited success and it was clear that they needed a star name and a decent engine to go with their potentially excellent chassis. Tyrrell was introduced to the general manager of Matra Sports and a deal was eventually done for Ken to run Matra-BRM Formula Two cars for Stewart in 1966.

Stewart became increasingly unhappy at BRM, and when Tyrrell spoke of moving up to Grand Prix racing in 1968 he was prepared to listen. He trusted Tyrrell's judgement since the former lumber merchant's brand of common sense contrasted sharply with the blustering pontification of the pompous boss at BRM. Even so, Tyrrell's plans were a touch uncertain. For a start, he had no chassis and no money. But he knew where to go for engines.

Tyrrell had visited the 1967 Dutch Grand Prix, a race which marked the debut of the Ford-Cosworth DFV engine. When the Ford powered the winning Lotus of Jim Clark across the line Tyrrell's enthusiasm knew no bounds, even though his resources could not stretch to the £7,500 necessary for a DFV. Determined to somehow put together a package for the following season, Tyrrell returned home and promptly ordered not one but three of the new engines. Then he spoke to Stewart, got his agreement – and promised to pay his salary with another £20,000 which he did not have.

Strictly speaking, the engines were not for sale, but Tyrrell not only talked Ford into reversing their decision, he persuaded them to guarantee Stewart's retainer as well! Together, Stewart and Tyrrell then worked on Dunlop and convinced the tyre company

TYRRELL

that this was the perfect opportunity for the British firm to revive their flagging reputation in motor racing. Dunlop agreed to put £80,000 into the empty kitty, thus allowing the £20,000 to be returned to Ford, leaving £60,000 for Ken to go racing in 1968. The only remaining problem was the absence of a decent chassis. Ken immediately thought of Matra. His timing could not have been better.

Thanks to Matra's success in the junior formulas, the French government had become interested in the prospect of bolstering national prestige through Grand Prix racing. A state oil company known as Elf had recently been created and motor sport was an obvious way to promote the image. With help from a state grant, plans were laid for an Elf-Matra Formula One programme which included not just the chassis but a brand-new V12 engine as well. It was a major undertaking, and as time went by there were worries within Matra that the project might not be seen to be giving the taxpayers an adequate return on their investment.

Enter Ken Tyrrell with a top driver, an excellent engine and Dunlop tyres. Yes, of course: Matra would be delighted to let Ken have one or two chassis at no charge! That way, Matra could hedge their bets. Indeed, Elf would come in as co-sponsor. The Tyrrell Grand Prix team – to be known for the time being as Equipe Matra International – was up and running.

Because the first Grand Prix of the 1968 season had been scheduled for 2 January, there had not been enough time to build the new Formula One car. Tyrrell was given an interim chassis which was basically a beefed-up Formula Two car, decorated in nothing more than dull green primer, and hacked about at the rear to accept the Ford DFV. Stewart put the ugly car on the front row of the grid and actually led the first lap. An engine problem brought retirement not long after – but a point had been made.

The definitive Matra-Ford car might have been finished in time for a non-championship event at Brands Hatch in March but, according to Stewart, major handling problems suggested it was far from ready to race. Stewart himself was not fit to race in the next two Grands Prix in Spain and Monaco after injuring his wrist during a Formula Two race. His place was taken initially by Jean-Pierre Beltoise, the Frenchman idle while waiting for Matra to make ready their own car with its V12 engine. Beltoise led briefly in Spain before an oil leak provoked a lengthy pit stop. He returned to set the fastest lap of the race and finish fifth.

With the works Matra ready for Monaco, Tyrrell chose the evocatively named Johnny Servoz-Gavin as Stewart's substitute for this important race. Servoz-Gavin, with his good looks and flowing blond hair, stunned the opposition when he put Ken's car on the front row of the grid. Despite stern warnings from Tyrrell about the peril of going too fast too

◄◄ *Mika Salo contemplates another retirement during a period of rebuilding*

Quiet days at Tyrrell but the British team has had its moments ▶

178 **TYRRELL**

soon on such a tight circuit, Servoz-Gavin got carried away as he led this prestigious Grand Prix. The Tyrrell clipped a guard rail and broke the transmission on the fourth lap. But there was no doubt now about the seriousness of Tyrrell's intentions. Rivals viewed Stewart's return with some trepidation.

Jackie qualified the Tyrrell-Matra on the front row of the grid in Belgium. He then led the majority of the laps on the fearsome road circuit at Spa-Francorchamps before a fuel pick-up problem snatched away a certain victory. It was only a matter of time before Tyrrell achieved the impossible. And, poignantly, he would do it on the circuit where the seeds had been sown twelve months before by that maiden victory for the Ford-Cosworth.

In a wet race at Zandvoort in Holland, Stewart led all but three laps to bring Tyrrell his first Formula One victory. Matra's day was made complete when Beltoise brought the

Oriental influence:

Ukyo Katayama ▼

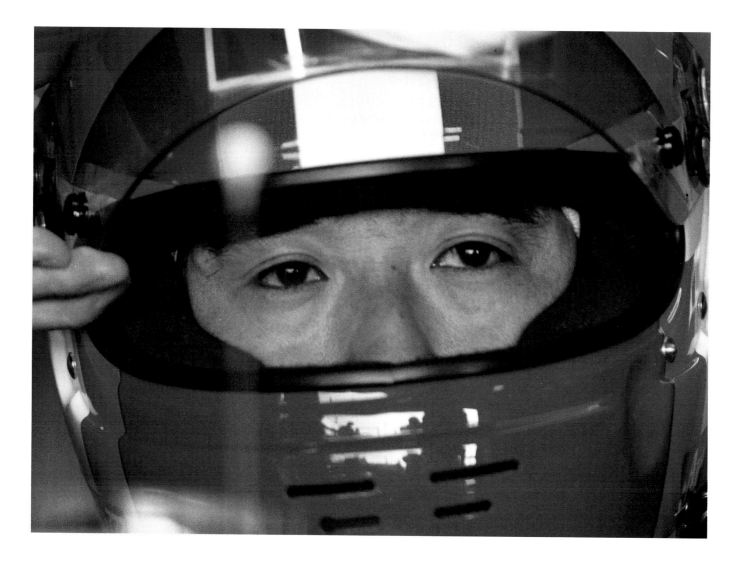

works car home in second place. Stewart and Tyrrell briefly lost form in France and Britain but Jackie more than made up for that in Germany with one of the most memorable drives of his career.

Racing on the fourteen-mile-long Nürburgring was difficult enough at the best of times. But when it was wet and misty, as it was throughout the Grand Prix weekend in 1968, it took bravery and skill of the highest order to defeat not just the opposition but the circuit itself. Stewart won by four minutes. He was out of the car and waiting on the podium by the time the third-place car had appeared through the gloom.

Tyrrell has always inspired impressive loyalty from those who work for him. His straight-talking ways are appreciated. You know where you are with Ken, even if at times he can be forcefully blunt and deliver what is known as a 'Tyrrell froth job', a reference to the saliva-riddled lecture. Certainly, his drivers were never placed on a pedestal. They were paid to do a job, just like everyone else in the team. Perhaps his ability to keep egos in check is best illustrated by an incident during practice for that race in Germany.

Stewart, having battled with the appalling elements, returned to the pits and switched off his engine. He was far from happy with his lot and he didn't care who knew it. Flipping open his visor and pulling down his flameproof face mask, Stewart began to recite a catalogue of problems: the handling of the car, the bumps, the dangers, the absence of grip, the futility of it all.

Tyrrell, standing beside the car with his clipboard tucked under his arm, listened impassively until the speech had ended. Then he leaned into the cockpit. 'You think you've got problems,' he roared. 'England are eighty-six for six!' He was almost joking.

It was a regular occurrence, when things were quiet at races close to Britain, to find Tyrrell sitting in his road car, fiddling with the radio and attempting to tune into BBC Long Wave. His team came first, of course. But the progress of the England XI ran it a close second.

Later that year British motor racing fans would be sitting by their radios waiting to hear if Ken's team had managed to defy all odds by winning the world championship at the first attempt. By dint of victory in the penultimate round in the United States Stewart was in the running as the season moved to its climax in Mexico. A blocked fuel pump put paid to his race and the title.

There was no doubt, however, that the Tyrrell–Stewart partnership would be in the reckoning in 1969, particularly when Matra produced a much-improved car. Stewart won six times, including victory at Silverstone at the end of a truly epic battle with the Lotus of his friend Jochen Rindt. By September, Stewart and Tyrrell had wrapped up

Tyrrell has always inspired impressive loyalty from those who work for him

An absence of sponsorship in 1996 has not helped Tyrrell recapture past form ▶▶

the championship, an amazing feat for a small team which was still operating out of Tyrrell's former timber yard, down in the woods at Ockham. City politics, however, were about to intervene.

Matra had been taken over by Chrysler, the parent company insisting that if Tyrrell wished to continue with the French chassis maker then a Matra V12 would have to replace the Ford engine. Following a test session in France, Stewart was totally convinced that the Ford DFV remained the better bet. There was no alternative for the new World Champions but to go shopping for a new car. And, naturally, none of the existing teams wanted to sell their products to a combination as potent as Tyrrell and Stewart.

There was one exception. March Engineering had been formed a few months before by four men with differing motor racing backgrounds, their united intention being to make and sell racing cars. Their plans were ambitious, to say the least. March produced cars for Formula Three and Formula Two, as well as designed and building a Grand Prix car. They could hardly believe their luck when Ken Tyrrell suddenly became a prospective client for a fairly standard car which had the outstanding benefit of the Ford-Cosworth engine. But Tyrrell was under no illusions. This would be nothing more than a stop-gap measure.

Having been snookered by politics, Ken knew the only satisfactory way to control his team's destiny would be by building his own cars, although the project would have to be kept secret in order not to compromise the working relationship with March Engineering. But before he could do anything, he had to find a suitable designer.

The previous year he had met a transmission expert working for Ferguson, an Englishman by the name of Derek Gardner. Because of his low profile, Gardner would be ideal, and by good fortune he was thinking of leaving Ferguson to go freelance. The thought of designing a Grand Prix car appealed enormously to the quiet-spoken Midlander. Agreement was reached in February 1970.

Gardner lived in Leamington Spa and this would become the birthplace of the Tyrrell Formula One car. A bedroom in the Gardner home was converted to a drawing office, the brief being to design a car which would be simple yet effective – and it had to be ready by the following August, an order which would be out of the question today, given the complexities of the modern Formula One car.

Gardner built a wooden mock-up of the chassis in his garage and Stewart flew to Warwickshire to try it for size. Such was the high level of secrecy involved that Gardner's daughter, an avowed Jackie Stewart fan, did not discover until some time later that her hero had actually been standing in the kitchen of her home.

The car proper eventually took shape at Ockham and the Formula One world was

stunned when Tyrrell-Ford 001 was rolled out on 17 August. In a business riddled with gossip and speculation, the fact that someone had actually managed to build a car – a major task which included the cooperation of many outside firms manufacturing components – without the slightest hint of a rumour was an achievement as notable as the car itself. As far as Tyrrell and Stewart were concerned, it had not come a moment too soon.

Even though Stewart had managed to win in Spain, the March had been desperately uncompetitive. When asked if he wished to try the Tyrrell at the remaining four races, Stewart did not hesitate. He led in Canada and in the United States before the inevitable teething troubles had their say. But the potential was there for all to see, making it relatively simple for Ken to finalize his sponsorship plans for 1971. Elf would begin a long-term association, signified by the new title, Elf Team Tyrrell.

The previous year Stewart had been joined by François Cevert, a tall Frenchman whose dark-eyed gypsy looks captivated women and charmed everyone he met. At first Cevert's driving had been inconsistent, but during 1971 he began to benefit from the influence of his masterly team-mate. The Tyrrell twins finished first and second in France and Germany, Stewart adding four more wins to give the Scotsman his second title, Cevert rounding off the year by scoring his first victory at Watkins Glen. It was a brilliant season by any standards.

As so often happens in motor racing, things did not run quite so smoothly the following year. 1972 began with a win for Stewart in Argentina but he would not see the top of the podium again for quite some time. A stomach ulcer forced him to miss one race and further time was lost with the development of Gardner's second car, Tyrrell 005. Stewart lost the championship, but when he won the final two races of the season it was clear that he would be the man to beat in 1973.

It would indeed be a vintage year but one which ended in terrible tragedy. Stewart was on peak form, driving superbly to secure his third championship with five victories. On three occasions – and at the daunting Nürburgring in particular – Cevert sat right with his team leader; proof that the Frenchman had matured enormously and was ready to adopt the role of number one driver when Jackie retired at the end of the season. The final race of 1973 was at Watkins Glen, which by chance would be Stewart's hundredth Grand Prix. That turned out to be the only happy coincidence associated with the weekend in autumnal New York State. During practice, Cevert crashed heavily and was killed instantly.

It was a desperate blow for a team which had seemed destined to continue where Stewart had left off. Now Tyrrell faced 1974 with two young and inexperienced drivers:

It would indeed be a vintage year but one which ended in terrible tragedy

Jody Scheckter and Patrick Depailler. The tide which had swept him to such wonderful times had suddenly turned. He would never enjoy consistent supremacy again.

Despite scoring a one-two in Sweden, and Scheckter winning the British Grand Prix, 1974 was a lean season for Tyrrell. 1975 was even worse, victory for Scheckter at his home Grand Prix in South Africa the only highlight. Meanwhile, Tyrrell and Derek Gardner had been scheming another surprise.

In an attempt to find an unusual performance advantage, Gardner dreamed up a car with six wheels, the four small wheels at the front minimizing the aerodynamic drag. Once again, Tyrrell somehow achieved complete secrecy even though the project involved Goodyear in the manufacture of tyres specially designed to fit the tiny wheels. If the Formula One media had been stunned by the appearance of the first Tyrrell car, they were gobsmacked when Ken unveiled the six-wheeler in the garden of his home.

Did the idea work? Yes and no. Tyrrell scored another one-two in Sweden in 1976 and no less than seven second places hinted at the potential. But it was not enough to prevent Scheckter from leaving at the end of the year, his place being taken by the immensely talented Ronnie Peterson. In the event, the best efforts of the Swedish driver could not coax a single victory for Tyrrell in 1977, the first year the team had been without a win. The six-wheeler, heavy and unwieldy, was ultimately defeated by its own complexity.

Two feet and six wheels ▶

▲ *A connection with Elf remains in 1996*

Peterson moved on and Derek Gardner returned to industry but there was fresh hope with the arrival of Didier Pironi, a young French driver, and Maurice Phillippe, a designer who had established a considerable reputation with Lotus. A more traditional four-wheeler, Tyrrell-Ford 008, was ready for 1978 and the loyal Depailler took his first Grand Prix win at Monaco, a timely victory which justified Elf's continuing sponsorship with Tyrrell – at least for the time being. Elsewhere in the paddock, however, designers had been getting to grips with the 'ground effect' aerodynamic phenomenon and Tyrrell was being left behind. At the end of 1978, Depailler left the team – as did Elf and another prime sponsor, Citicorp.

Tyrrell, in his usual determined style, pressed on. He signed another Frenchman, Jean-Pierre Jarier, and Phillippe designed a ground effect car, Tyrrell-Ford 009. With nothing on the car but the maker's name, Tyrrell managed to get by until securing support from Candy Domestic Appliances in May 1979. There were no decent results to speak of and the Italian backers remained faithful through 1980 and pinned their hopes

on Tyrrell 010. The best results were a couple of fourth places – and a new altitude record.

Pironi had moved to Ligier, his place being taken by Derek Daly, the Irishman making an impact in every sense when he misjudged his braking at the first corner at Monaco, launched himself off the back of another car, his Tyrrell then executing a novel airborne overtaking manoeuvre before landing on the back of his team-mate's car. Such an instant wipeout was typical of Tyrrell's fortune; 'pathetic' was how Ken succinctly summed up the 1980 season. In actual fact, Tyrrell had finished sixth in the Constructors' Championship. It may have been his worst result since arriving in Formula One, but compared with what lay in store, it should have been cause for celebration.

Candy took their money elsewhere and, once again, Tyrrell returned to a hand-to-mouth existence. The financial drought would last for the best part of two seasons, Tyrrell cutting his cloth by reducing his workforce from forty-five to thirty-three. There was a resurgence of sorts with the arrival of Michele Alboreto in 1982. A well-deserved win at the final race in Las Vegas helped secure Benetton, then testing the temperature of Formula One, as a team sponsor. It was the boost Tyrrell needed, the increased funding allowing much-needed development. But at the end of 1983 there was just one victory to show for their efforts and, once again, the support began to crumble. Alboreto moved to Ferrari, and at a time when the leading teams were switching to turbocharged engines Tyrrell had to continue with the trusty Ford-Cosworth. On the plus side, however, he signed a couple of young chargers, Martin Brundle and Stefan Bellof, these two hurling the nimble little cars in pursuit of their more powerful rivals.

Nothing will match the desperate low of being thrown out of the 1984 championship

Ken Tyrrell has coped with many setbacks over the years but nothing will match the desperate low of being thrown out of the 1984 championship because of alleged irregularities on his car. It was no coincidence that he had been standing in the way of legislation designed to suit turbocharging – as used by the vast majority of teams – but the public perception of such a devastating indictment by the sport's politically motivated governing body would cause deep hurt in such an honourable man.

It was typical of his luck that Bellof, whom Ken considered to be the greatest driver he had come across since Stewart, was killed in a sports car race in 1985, the year Tyrrell finally switched to turbocharging with a Renault V6. For the next few seasons he would struggle, sponsors and drivers coming and going with little effect. In 1988, one of the worst years on record for Tyrrell, his team would score just five points in total, the absence of finance completely stifling development. It must also be said that the car that year was one of the least competitive the team had ever produced. It was so bad that Jonathan Palmer and Julian Bailey failed to qualify twelve times, an appalling record for

the team and a bleak score which effectively wrecked Bailey's Formula One career. With Maurice Phillippe having long since departed, it was apparent that the technical side of the team was in desperate need of reorganization and updating.

The arrival of Dr Harvey Postlethwaite, the former Ferrari designer, brought new life and methods to the engineering department which seemed to be struggling in the dark ages. Similarly, the signing of Jean Alesi midway through 1989 raised the team's profile even further, particularly during the following season when Postlethwaite's new car lifted Tyrrell into fifth place in the Constructors' Championship. Not for the first time, however, the momentum soon disappeared, along with Postlethwaite, who went back to Ferrari for a brief period before returning to Tyrrell in 1993. Once again, Tyrrell had to begin the slow and very difficult climb back to competitiveness.

◀ *The struggle
continues . . .*

Throughout this roller-coaster ride spanning more than twenty-five seasons, the Tyrrell workforce has remained intensely loyal. The Tyrrell Racing Organisation, despite its grand title and the recent technical advances down at Ockham, remains essentially a family team. Ken and his wife, Norah, attend every race. Norah's role as time-keeper and sandwich-maker may have been lost to modern technology and the impressive catering which is an essential part of any team these days, but Ken maintains an active interest in pit lane activities, his headset clamped around that familiar craggy face. Bob Tyrrell looks after sponsorship activities, a field which has provided a depth of experience for Ken's youngest son, given the many backers which have passed across the flanks of various Tyrrell cars over the years.

The bad days were difficult, sometimes appallingly so; the best days very good, sometimes totally brilliant. And yet, Ken Tyrrell has remained exactly the same; always a fine man to have around in a 'good bloke' sort of way, regardless of the circumstances. His cackling good humour is unwavering, his frothing enthusiasm inexhaustible. He has needed to make full call on both.

WILLIAMS

WILLIAMS

WILLIAMS

DRIVERS:

DAMON HILL (ENGLAND)

JACQUES VILLENEUVE (CANADA)

TEAM PRINCIPAL • FRANK WILLIAMS

CHIEF DESIGNER • PATRICK HEAD/ADRIAN NEWEY

CAR • WILLIAMS FW18

ENGINE • RENAULT V10

FIRST GRAND PRIX • ARGENTINA, 1973

GRANDS PRIX CONTESTED • 346

WINS • 83

Williams Grand Prix Engineering is a product of motor racing in the Sixties. It was founded on the dreams and ambitions of one man at a time when anything seemed possible. Ask Frank Williams to contemplate such an adventure today and he laughs at the very thought. Having won five World Driver's titles and seven Constructors' Championships, Frank's humble beginnings belong to another world. And yet it is the same resourcefulness and tenacity which continues to underpin everything at Williams, making them the most consistently successful Formula One team across a span of seventeen years.

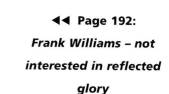

◄◄ **Page 192:**
Frank Williams – not interested in reflected glory

The accumulated experience and wealth has been recycled; nothing has been wasted. At the beginning of 1996, the Williams headquarters moved to a thirty-two-acre site near the village of Grove in Oxfordshire. The spacious reception area alone is larger than the garage and lock-ups where Frank Williams began his business in 1968. But the impressive accoutrements necessary for success nearly three decades later merely reflect the same almost excruciating desire to win which has carried Williams through lean and sometimes desperate times.

Frank Williams is a 'racer'. The term is applied to someone who loves and understands motor sport. A racer is an enthusiast working in the business who appreciates that it is sometimes necessary to sacrifice business logic and financial common sense for the sake of winning. Finishing second in order to show a profit is unacceptable to a racer. Winning at all costs is the only way.

Frank Williams has taken his fair share of risks over the years

Of course, when operating at the top level of Grand Prix racing rampant profligacy is neither desirable nor the easy solution, particularly when shouldering the responsibility for more than 220 employees. But there must be a sense of adventure and a willingness to gamble. These days, the Williams team may be rather more conservative than some, although Frank Williams has taken his fair share of risks over the years. One of them almost killed him.

Rushing to Nice airport after the final test session before the start of the 1986 season, he lost control of his car and crashed into a field. As his hire car began a series of rolls, the windscreen pillar on the driver's side collapsed. Williams has been a tetraplegic ever since.

It was a devastating blow in every sense, particularly for a fitness fanatic who could scarcely sit still for five minutes and who took daily runs and competed regularly in marathons. And yet there is not a trace of self-pity. It is almost as if he half expected to fly off the road at some point in his life, such was his love of driving quickly. Certainly, the accident came as no surprise to those who knew Frank and had seen him compete in saloon cars and single-seater racing cars in the early Sixties. They were deeply shocked

Sponsors pay handsomely to be associated with Williams ▶

Jacques Villeneuve is the focus of attention on pole position for the 1996 Australian Grand Prix ▶▶

WILLIAMS 195

WILLIAMS

by the consequences – particularly when his life lay in the balance during the critical few weeks which followed – but, in truth, his friends knew the crash was inevitable.

Frank's progress on the racetracks had been very promising on occasions, but more often than not dramatically erratic. He was part of a happy-go-lucky band of young racers, most of whom were wealthy enough to spend their summers touring Europe, going from minor race meeting to minor race meeting in search of competition, some decent starting money and, if they were lucky, the bonus of prize money.

The racing machines, usually Formula Three cars, were slung onto trailers and towed anywhere between Sweden and Sicily. It was a hand-to-mouth existence – one which would not survive in today's more professional and sponsorship-orientated climate – and such an exciting way of life appealed enormously to Frank Williams. He could scarcely contain his enthusiasm for fast motoring, but the deciding factor in the end was a realization of his personal limitations and the absence of cash. The final crunch came, quite literally, in 1966 when he crashed his Brabham on a level crossing while racing in Portugal.

If nothing else, however, he was fiercely ambitious. He had learned how to wheel and deal as a means of survival. He bought and sold racing cars and handled spare parts with such success that his business gathered momentum to the exclusion of everything else, even a deep desire to finally purge competitive driving from his system by returning to the wheel with a proper budget. The formation of Frank Williams (Racing Cars) Ltd. in 1968 led to a career as an entrant and an eventual championship status which were beyond even Frank's wildest dreams. Well, almost.

Frank's unfettered ambitions were charged by his association with Piers Courage, scion of the brewing family and the epitome of a dashing young man of the Sixties. Courage had taken up racing against the wishes of his parents, with mixed results; a reputation for crashing outweighed the occasional brilliant drive. But Williams was convinced about such latent talent and he offered Courage a drive in a Formula Three car which Frank happened to own at the time. Not only did Piers race with flair and aggression, Williams was so enthused by the performance of his friend that he decided to become Courage's entrant.

It quickly developed into an extremely close partnership despite Courage's privileged background and Williams' working-class upbringing in the North-East. Williams was not alone in finding Courage an engaging and charming fellow and he was easily persuaded to take the plunge and invest in a Formula Two Brabham for the 1968 season. It cost Williams £10,000. Today that wouldn't pay the team's hotel bill at a Grand Prix. But in 1968, it was money Williams did not have.

Robbing Peter to pay Paul, using this year's income to settle last year's bills, Williams and Courage raced headlong down a road which, whether they liked it or not, was leading to Grand Prix racing and the purchase of a Brabham Formula One car. Courage had already made a less than brilliant Formula One debut with the BRM team, but since he continued to show flashes of inspiration with Williams there seemed no point in stopping the exciting sequence of events, even if Frank's bank manager could scarcely see the logic.

Strictly speaking, the latest Grand Prix models were not available off the shelf, certainly not when the purchaser was capable of entering a driver who could threaten the works cars. As it turned out, the 1969 Brabham had been changed very little from the previous year's car. Quietly and discreetly, Frank Williams got his hands on a 1968 model which had been sold to someone who had promised to use the car for purposes other than Grand Prix racing. Jack Brabham was not pleased when he found out – and he was definitely not amused when Courage, at the end of a stunning drive, beat the triple World Champion into second place in the money-rich United States Grand Prix.

Courage was now a serious prospect and Williams had to find him a car for 1970. Frank had come into contact with Alessandro de Tomaso, a charismatic Argentinian who was manufacturing his own sports cars in a bid to challenge Ferrari and Lamborghini in the high-performance sector of the market place. Such were his persuasive powers that he convinced Williams of the merit in the de Tomaso company building a Formula One car which Williams would then prepare and enter. It was an exclusive liaison which, although attractive on paper, would have tragic consequences on 21 June.

On the twenty-fourth lap of the Dutch Grand Prix, Courage crashed and perished in the ensuing inferno. Williams was devastated. To have his passionate if sometimes naive dreams ended in this way was one thing. To lose such a dear friend in the process was quite another.

But the alliance with de Tomaso was effectively over and Williams reached the end of the year with more debts than assets. Using borrowed funds from friends, he struggled on by racing a car bought from March, a commercially-minded company more interested in results on the balance sheet than on the racetrack. Frank's cause was not helped by the need to keep repairing the March, either because it had broken through appalling unreliability or because the drivers kept crashing.

For 1972, Frank was tempted by the £40,000 on offer from Politoys, a company making model cars, to build a Grand Prix car to carry the Italian firm's name. Contracting out the chassis manufacture to a specialist company in Surrey, Williams had to wait until mid-season before the new car was ready. Then his driver, Henri Pescarolo from

There seemed no point in stopping the exciting sequence of events, even if Frank's bank manager could scarcely see the logic

WILLIAMS

▲ Williams Formula One cars have come a long way during the past twenty years

France, promptly stuffed the Politoys into a bank during the first lap of the British Grand Prix.

Things went from bad to worse during the next few seasons, and Williams operated on the verge of bankruptcy at a time when sponsorship was getting into its stride. Support from the likes of John Player and Marlboro lifted teams such as Lotus and McLaren onto a different level from Frank's shoestring collection of second-rate equipment raced by drivers whose meagre financial offerings often outweighed their supposed talent. The unfettered optimism of racing with Piers Courage seemed an age away.

◀ *Villeneuve: another link between Williams and Canada*

Always on the alert for any business opportunity, Williams latched on to Walter Wolf, a hard-headed Austro-Canadian who had made millions in the oil business. Wolf wanted to play at motor racing and he began 1975 by giving Williams desperately needed support. By the end of the season he had effectively bought the company. Frank Williams (Racing Cars) Ltd. became Walter Wolf Racing and Frank remained a part of it by running the team. But it wasn't *his* team.

For 1977, he decided to go it alone once more. Williams Grand Prix Engineering (WGPE) was formed. Finally, at the age of thirty-five, Francis Owen Garbett Williams was on a long, straight and fast road to success. And joining him for this exciting phase was Patrick Head, a designer who would pen the world-beating Williams cars.

They had met at the end of 1975. Williams had been looking for an engineer prior to the Wolf takeover, Patrick joining the new liaison only to find twelve months later that Frank was attempting to persuade him to leave Wolf and join WGPE. It was a tricky

200 **WILLIAMS**

decision because Wolf's streamlined and adequately financed operation was impressive whereas Frank's record was . . . not impressive.

Williams was determined to get it right this time. To see him on his way, Frank had to resort once more to buying a car from March and relying on help from one or two wealthy friends to see him through this difficult period while, at the same time, planning long-term on a grand scale.

The first hint of it came during the 1977 season when the March carried a small amount of identification for Saudia, the airline of the Kingdom of Saudi Arabia. Through his relentless efforts to find proper support, Frank had become the first team owner to tap into the rich vein of Saudi sponsorship. Plans for Head to design the first Williams car were accelerated.

Williams had set up shop in a small industrial unit at Station Road in Didcot with a staff of no more than ten people. In December 1977, the British motor sport press were invited to Station Road to see the first Williams car, FW06. But the occasion, which appeared low-key and relaxed, had more to it than that. The neat white car with green flashes carried nothing but Saudi sponsorship identification. Late in the morning, the beat of a helicopter landing on a nearby football pitch announced the arrival of the director of Saudia Airlines and three board members. Greeted by a beaming, besuited Frank

The gloves are off . . . ▶

Williams, they had come to inspect their car. And among the welcoming party was its driver, Alan Jones.

Williams and Head had chosen the Australian partly because the narrow choice left them with no alternative, partly because he had shown promise in his limited number of Grand Prix outings – including a win in Austria the previous year – and partly because he was a no-nonsense racer who spoke the same direct language as his new employers. Williams Grand Prix Engineering was, at last, ready to go racing in the proper manner. And sooner than Frank had expected.

At the second race of the 1978 season in Brazil, Jones hurled the simple but effective little car onto eighth place on the grid. Two races later at Long Beach he was thinking about challenging for the lead when the nose wings broke. This was to be part of a difficult learning process as a system of production checks was gradually implemented on the back of each painful lesson. But by the end of the season, WGPE had scored 11 championship points. Frank had started the season hoping, as he put it at the time, 'just to hang in there, qualify near the back of the grid and maybe finish races'. Instead, his team had become truly competitive. Williams Grand Prix Engineering would never look back.

Patrick Head had become a full partner in the team, a matter of mere nomenclature for such a pragmatist. His thoughts were on other things, and from his drawing board would emerge Williams FW07, destined to be one of the most successful Formula One cars of all time.

Due to continuing limited resources, in both finance and manpower, the new car would not emerge until the 1979 season was under way. At its second race – the Belgian Grand Prix at Zolder – Jones led for fourteen laps before being sidelined by electrical trouble. It was the first time a Williams-entered car had headed the field since Courage in the Brabham ten years before; it was the first time ever for a car bearing Frank's own name.

It was clear to everyone in this small but highly motivated team that the good times were just around the corner. In keeping with standard Formula One practice, Williams were now entering two cars for each race; the second was driven by Clay Regazzoni, an experienced and genial Swiss, a 'racer' in every sense who fitted perfectly into the team. Regazzoni was employed as an able back-up for Jones, and Clay's absence of ego was such that he could handle the role with ease. It paid off handsomely at Monaco when Jones crashed out and Regazzoni drove a dogged race to finish second.

It seemed a victory could not be far away and the British Grand Prix at Silverstone was as good a place as any to do it. Jones took pole position in brilliant style. He led with

▲ *The Williams-Renault FW18, the latest in a long line of successful cars from Williams Grand Prix Engineering*

ease – until a mechanical failure intervened. But Regazzoni was there to take up the laurels and give Frank Williams his first Grand Prix win.

It was a hugely popular victory. Clay, with his wide grin and bandit moustache, was adored by the crowds and there was understandable delight the length and breath of Silverstone for Frank Williams. After all his trials and tribulations over the years, to score his first win at home was a story heaped with emotion. Typically, Frank was more concerned about Jones having lost.

Now WGPE was rolling. Jones's day would come two weeks later in Germany, where he scored the first of three wins on the trot. By the season's end, the Australian had four victories to his credit and third place in the championship; the team finished second in the constructors' series.

Williams were ready for 1980. £40,000 alone was spent on a pre-season test session lasting a week in Argentina; Frank would have been stunned if such a thing had been suggested just five years before. FW07 had been improved; it was a winner – on paper.

In reality, it took time to make the revised car work properly. Jones won the opening race of the season but the team was under no illusions. The battle for the championship ebbed and flowed. First Renault, with their turbocharged engine, looked like being the most consistent challenger. Then the French team Ligier. Finally, in the second half of the season, came a more serious and consistent attack from Brabham and their Brazilian driver Nelson Piquet.

The championship boiled down to a tense shoot-out between Jones and Piquet in Canada. They collided at the first corner; the race was stopped. At the restart, Piquet led. Then his engine blew up. Jones won the race – and the World Championship. Williams Grand Prix Engineering were Constructors' Champions for the first time. And to round off the season, Williams finished first and second in the final race at Watkins Glen in the United States, scene of that great drive by Piers Courage eleven years before. Frank could not have been more satisfied, or proud. He had worked assiduously for his success. Now came the hard part. Having reached the top, he had to try and stay there.

In 1981, Grand Prix was wracked with political controversy which threatened to split the sport in two. Harmony, of a sort, finally prevailed but Jones's chances of retaining his title were spoilt by reliability problems and the occasional driving error. Regazzoni had been dropped at the beginning of the previous year, Carlos Reutemann taking his place. On his day, Reutemann could be brilliant. Unfortunately, those days would be few and far between.

He was consistent, however, and won championship points in sixteen consecutive races. That impressive run would eventually come to an end but when the season reached its halfway point he had done enough to hold a commanding seventeen-point lead of the championship. He then proceeded to fritter away his advantage. Going into the final race at Las Vegas he led Piquet by one point, but on the day offered no resistance whatsoever. Williams at least had the consolation of taking the Constructors' Championship.

Revelling in the stifling heat of Nevada, Jones had destroyed the opposition. It was a fine way to end his last race before retiring but, regrettably, he devalued such an impressive exit by making an ill-advised return a few years later.

His late decision to quit had left Frank Williams with few options. He chose Keke Rosberg, a chain-smoking Finn with an extrovert style and enough aggression to keep Reutemann – now the number one at Williams – on his toes. Williams was just coming to terms with his revised driver line-up when, after two races, he received another shock. Reutemann suddenly decided to retire. Williams saw out the rest of the year with

Rosberg and Derek Daly, an Irishman who failed to deliver the results expected of him. Rosberg, in fact, provided Williams with just one victory in 1982, but in a topsy-turvy season when eleven different drivers won races it was enough to give the jaunty Scandinavian the championship.

Rosberg remained for 1983, Daly made way for the Frenchman Jacques Laffite but, more importantly, the Williams team were about to undergo changes in other departments. It became clear that a turbocharged engine was the thing to have. Ever since the start of his Formula One campaign, Frank Williams had used the Ford-Cosworth V8, a hugely reliable engine but being non-turbocharged now short on power. Nevertheless, Rosberg used it to brilliant effect at Monaco – a circuit where engine power is not at a premium – and gave the team their only victory of the 1983 season.

Long-term planning was in evidence when, later in the year, Williams began a highly successful alliance with Honda and their turbocharged V6. It would take time for the combination to gel and it was left to Rosberg's tenacity on a crumbling track surface in Dallas to provide the single win for Williams in 1984. By the start of the following year, however, the Williams-Honda was ready to take on all comers. And, to help them do it, Williams signed Nigel Ernest James Mansell, one of the most controversially brilliant drivers of the decade.

Damon Hill: signed by Williams for a song ▶

At the time, Mansell was seen by the rest of the paddock as a liability. He was quick on occasions but seemed to spend the rest of his time either crashing or moaning. Williams was sure Nigel had the potential, if only it could be harnessed. It was ironic therefore that Mansell should blossom within a team which, having grown up with the forcefully independent ways of Alan Jones, were not exactly noted for mollycoddling their drivers. True, Mansell had his incidents, but when he won his first grand prix, at Brands Hatch in October 1985, his confidence was charged. He won the next race, in South Africa, thus setting the scene for a highly dramatic season in 1986.

Rosberg left to join McLaren, his place being taking by Nelson Piquet, now twice a World Champion. There were no holds barred between the Williams drivers as they divided the spoils, Piquet winning in Brazil, Germany, Hungary and Italy, Mansell in Belgium, Canada, France, Britain and Portugal. Going into the final race in Australia, Williams had totally dominated the Constructors' Championship. But the driver's title was far from settled. Mansell and Piquet were neck and neck. And not far behind lurked the menacing presence of Alain Prost in his McLaren.

During the course of a gripping race on the streets of Adelaide, all three drivers took turns at looking as if they would win the title. Then, in one of the most memorable pieces of television, Mansell's left-rear tyre blew spectacularly on the back straight just as he

seemed poised to totally defy his many critics and achieve a lifetime's ambition. The Williams rattled to a halt, Piquet was called in for a precautionary tyre change and Prost drove serenely by to win the championship. Frank Williams, still coming to terms with the terrible consequences of his road accident eight months before, watched the denouement from a BBC television studio in London.

In 1987, Mansell and Piquet once again duelled for the title, but this time the dominance of the Williams-Honda was such that they had the battleground to themselves. The outcome was settled at the penultimate race when Mansell crashed during practice and invalided himself out of the rest of the season, leaving Williams and Piquet to lift both championships for the Didcot-based organization.

Things had moved on apace, the team having expanded and three years earlier moved to a purpose-built factory on the outskirts of the town. The chain of command Frank had put in place was impressive and the team had barely missed its stride in the aftermath of his accident. Patrick continued to direct technical affairs. As for poor Frank, the only positive thing to be said was that he happened to be out of action during the one period in the year when the team's commercial activities are traditionally at their

▲ *Renault eventually replaced Honda. Will the roles be reversed when Renault quit at the end of 1997?*

quietest, all contracts having been put in place for the forthcoming season. It didn't take long for the boss to return, an admirably stoic approach allowing him to carry on with the business he continued to love with such an intense passion.

In 1987 he had been forced to address the question of engines. Honda had, for reasons best known to themselves, decided to switch to McLaren, thus breaking a contract which had another year to run with Williams. A financial settlement was reached, and although miffed at the time, Williams were not unduly worried. In hindsight, it could not have begun to repair the damage wrought by the sudden departure. Turbos were being phased out in 1988; Frank and Patrick felt they had an adequate package with the non-turbo V8 built by John Judd in Rugby. Piquet left to join Lotus, his place being taken by Riccardo Patrese of Italy. Williams thought they might get by quite adequately. Some hope.

The McLaren-Honda won fifteen of the sixteen races in 1988. Williams, by comparison, posted retirement after retirement to finish a humble seventh in the Constructors' Championship. It would be the lowest point for Williams Grand Prix Engineering. Never mind getting by, the team's survival would be under threat if this continued.

Fortunately, Frank had been planning ahead as usual. Renault had abandoned Formula One at the end of 1985, the attempts by the motor manufacturer to run their own team having lost momentum after allowing the championship to slip from their grasp at the end of 1983. But Renault's engine department continued to work unobtrusively towards building an engine for the non-turbocharged formula due to be introduced in 1989. Williams persuaded Renault that they should supply him with the new V10.

Mansell went off to drive for Ferrari and Patrese was joined by Thierry Boutsen of Belgium. It would obviously take time for the Williams-Renault partnership to meld and, along the way, Boutsen won two races. There were two more wins in 1990, but this was hardly progress. It was time to bring back Nigel Mansell.

Frank had held discussions with Ayrton Senna, but when those fell through Mansell was the most obvious candidate, even though he had announced his retirement. He was easily persuaded. He would have number one status and £4.6 million to ease the pain of changing his mind. Head had brought in Adrian Newey to assist with the design of their 1991 contender. With Patrese on board for another year, this would be Mansell's best chance yet to win the title.

The Williams-Renault FW18. The best car of 1996 ▶

In a typically dramatic year in which he won five races, Mansell ultimately lost the title to Ayrton Senna due to a mixture of driving errors, mechanical problems and tactical mistakes by the team. But the potential was clearly there and the Englishman was re-signed for another season.

This time Mansell and Williams-Renault wiped the floor with the opposition. Nigel won five races in succession at the start of the season and claimed a record nine in total. He was World Champion by August and Williams had another Constructors' Championship to add to their impressive list. What could be better?

Quite a lot, according to Mansell. Unhappy that Williams should be talking to Alain Prost – and, on occasions, Ayrton Senna – about a drive for 1993, Mansell and Frank Williams engaged in a hard-headed debate over money and conditions. Discussions – if that is the correct word – reached such a frenetic state that Mansell, having rejected a reasonable offer early in the season, then found that he was being forced to take a pay cut. Relationships plunged from bad to worse and, in a typical fit of pique, he announced his retirement in September. There would be no going back. Prost would drive for Williams. Patrese, meanwhile, had wisely looked after his own interests and grabbed the opportunity to drive for Benetton. Once again, Frank and Patrick were searching for a driver. They had to look no further than their own back yard.

Damon Hill had been employed as test driver since 1991. Calm, analytical and

ambitious, the son of a former World Champion was seen as being worthy of a place on the race team as an understudy to Prost. It would prove to be an ideal partnership, particularly as the latest Williams had few serious rivals; Hill won his first Grand Prix in Hungary while Prost confirmed his status as pre-season favourite by collecting seven victories and the championship. Williams scooped the constructors' trophy for the sixth time. But Frank was not satisfied with that.

It had been his ambition to sign Ayrton Senna, regarded as the best driver of the day, if not all time. Frank finally achieved his goal, the downside being the departure of Prost: the two drivers, sworn enemies in the past, were unable to work together.

Senna was immediately marked down as favourite, but it would not be as simple as that. Far from it. 1994 turned out to be cataclysmic, not just for Williams but for the sport as a whole. During the opening laps of the San Marino Grand Prix Senna's car left the track and slammed into a concrete wall, ripping off the right front wheel. The force was such that a suspension arm penetrated Senna's crash helmet. He died of his injuries later that day.

The sport went into shock. But the racing had to continue. Hill suddenly found the responsibility of team leadership thrust upon him. What's more, the car, acting as if on a knife-edge, was difficult to drive. David Coulthard was elevated from test driver to number two, the Scotsman losing his drive on a couple of occasions thanks to an ill-starred and ill-advised comeback by Nigel Mansell.

Hill, meanwhile, was gathering his composure and his momentum. By the last race of the season he and Michael Schumacher were separated by just one point. In the race itself, they got too close, collided – and Schumacher won the championship. But Williams at least had the consolation of another Constructors' Championship. Hill vowed to settle the score in 1995.

At first he looked like doing it, but somehow the season degenerated into chaos. Hill and Schumacher collided twice, Hill coming off worst in the psychological battle which followed. Schumacher and Benetton went from strength to strength to collect both championships, leaving Williams with nothing to show except four wins for Hill and a maiden victory for Coulthard.

As ever, Frank Williams had been thinking ahead. In the autumn he revealed the bold move of signing the Indycar champion Jacques Villeneuve in place of Coulthard. Hill, meanwhile, returned to his home in Ireland for a long, hard think.

He returned, refreshed and revitalized. Williams had a car to match. Hill won three races in succession and the team regained its momentum and its reputation for consistent excellence. The Williams legend, born in another world, was continuing.

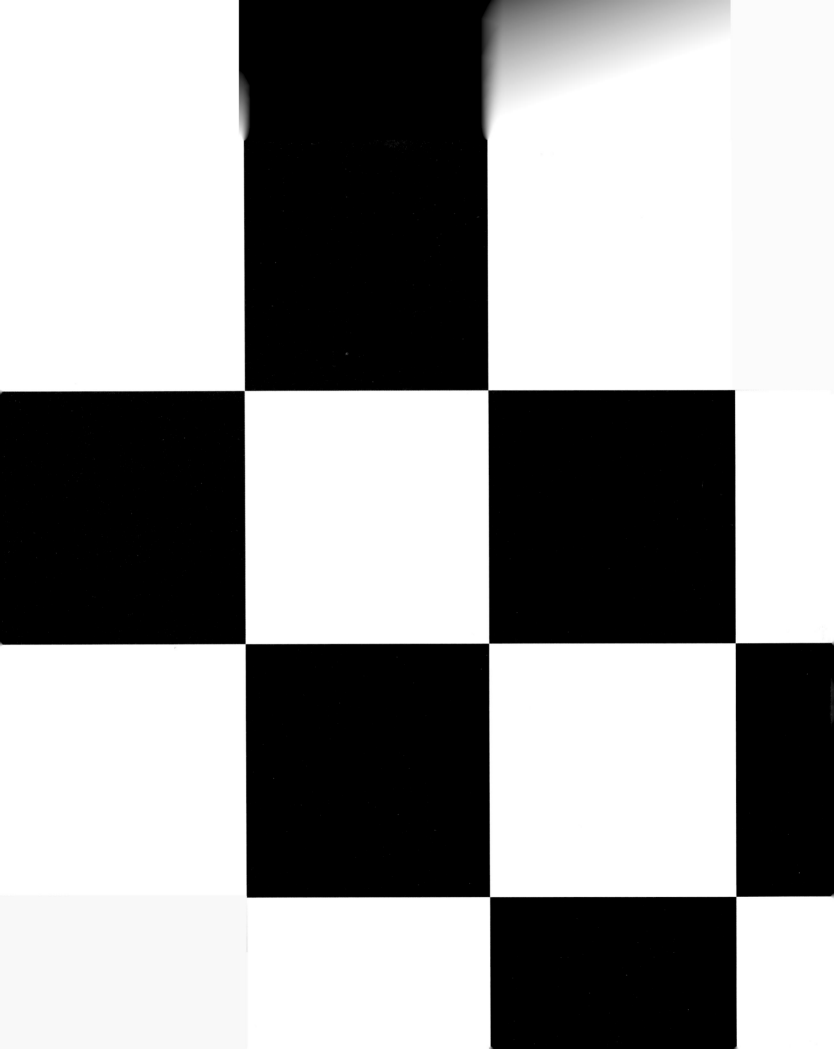